Praise for Jill Roe:

'Jill Roe writes elegantly and has assembled a promising cast of black-comedy characters . . . [With] her light touch and sense of mischief, she handles the quiet menace brewing below the surface with the poise and gently malicious enjoyment of a younger Muriel Spark, waiting to pounce.' *Literary Review*

'Jill Roe demonstrates how to place believable people oh-so-gently into the most unthreatening surroundings – and then to create a tension that builds and builds . . . a sensitive page-turner . . . clever, and quietly compelling.' *BBC Homes & Antiques*

'With her light touch and sense of mischief . . . Jill Roe writes elegantly and has assembled a promising cast of black-comedy characters' *Times Literary Supplement*

'Award winning author . . . Jill Roe has a charming descriptive writing talent which draws you into the world of Dove like a magnet' *Peterborough Evening Telegraph*

'an elegant, heart-warming comedy, shot through with sly humour' *The Daily Telegraph*

'Gently and elegantly written . . . [with] a very satisfying edge' *Northern Echo*

A Well Kept Secret

Jill Roe

FLAME
Hodder & Stoughton

Copyright © 1998 by Jill Roe

First published in 1998 by Hodder and Stoughton
First published in paperback in 1999 by Hodder and Stoughton
A division of Hodder Headline PLC
A Flame Paperback

The right of Jill Roe to be identified as the Author of
the Work has been asserted by her in accordance with the
Copyright, Designs and Patents Act 1988.

10 9 8 7 6 5 4 3 2 1

All characters in this publication are fictitious and any
resemblance to real persons, living or dead, is purely coincidental.

A CIP catalogue record for this book is available
from the British Library

ISBN 0 340 68279 5

Typeset by Palimpsest Book Production Limited,
Polmont, Stirlingshire
Printed and bound in Great Britain by
Caledonian International Book Manufacturing Ltd, Glasgow

Hodder and Stoughton
A division of Hodder Headline PLC
338 Euston Road
London NW1 3BH

For my sister Ann
who gave me the title

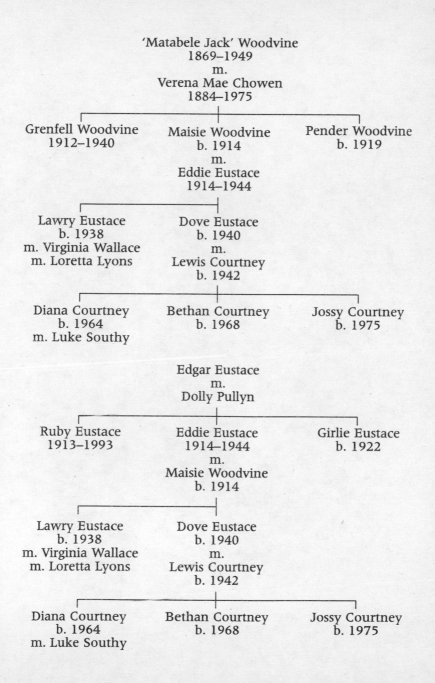

'Matabele Jack' Woodvine
1869–1949
m.
Verena Mae Chowen
1884–1975

Grenfell Woodvine
1912–1940

Maisie Woodvine
b. 1914
m.
Eddie Eustace
1914–1944

Pender Woodvine
b. 1919

Lawry Eustace
b. 1938
m. Virginia Wallace
m. Loretta Lyons

Dove Eustace
b. 1940
m.
Lewis Courtney
b. 1942

Diana Courtney
b. 1964
m. Luke Southy

Bethan Courtney
b. 1968

Jossy Courtney
b. 1975

Edgar Eustace
m.
Dolly Pullyn

Ruby Eustace
1913–1993

Eddie Eustace
1914–1944
m.
Maisie Woodvine
b. 1914

Girlie Eustace
b. 1922

Lawry Eustace
b. 1938
m. Virginia Wallace
m. Loretta Lyons

Dove Eustace
b. 1940
m.
Lewis Courtney
b. 1942

Diana Courtney
b. 1964
m. Luke Southy

Bethan Courtney
b. 1968

Jossy Courtney
b. 1975

1

Lewis Courtney woke gently, as he always did, music softly prising open his eyes, supporting him as he surfaced from sleep. The time on the clock-radio showed that it was still not seven and he knew without turning his head or moving an exploratory arm that Dove's side of the bed was empty.

Dove, watching him as she dressed quietly and tidied her hair, said, 'Maisie's waking earlier and earlier; I can't leave her lying there for hours on her own.' There was a silence, neither Lewis nor Dove willing to allow his grievance to become other than inconsequential, Dove almost believing what she had said, each of them knowing it to be a misrepresentation of the truth. Dove looked towards Lewis, his shape blurred against the grey light from the window. 'I'm sorry, Lewis, but you do understand don't you? We knew it might be like this when she came to live here.'

'Of course I understand,' Lewis said, 'On Hearing the First Cuckoo in Spring' playing softly in his ears. 'I'll have another half hour in bed, but I'll miss you.' He had turned on his back and was watching Dove while she dressed, her movements slower and heavier than they used to be but still graceful, a woman in middle age with responsibilities that encompassed her, circumscribing her day, allowing her no pretence of the independence which she had promised herself that one day she would seize and use to her advantage.

Dove touched her husband on the shoulder and walked through the quiet house to the kitchen, gathering Baffin and Mossy around her ankles as she unlocked the side door onto the garden. There was a door which led directly from the kitchen passage into that quarter of the house where Dove's mother lived, but Dove preferred to walk around the house to what had been the back door, reinforcing the pretence that Maisie and Maisie's brother Pender lived quite separate lives, proximity to Dove and Lewis just a happy coincidence.

The day was as soft and pale as an opal; trees and fields which Dove knew to be there, eclipsed just beyond her sight by mist and lingering dawn. The grass at the foot of the hedges glittered silver with dew, and a spider's web swung heavy with diamond drops strung between the gate and its supporting post, Dove disturbing it as she unclipped the catch before walking up the damp, grey slabs to Maisie's front door.

There had been hollyhocks in profusion along the wall of the house, double yellows and carmines, taller than the low windows on either side of the door. Now, Dove noticed with distaste, the remaining flowers were balls of brown slime, the heavy dews of autumn defeating their valiant struggle at a semblance of gaiety.

A straggle of Chinese lanterns had colonised a bed beside the path and Dove kicked them out of the way, pale stems like watery serpents reaching out towards her legs. Pools of cyclamen spread their pale wings under every tree, but the leaves on the shrubs were turning and falling and the garden looked disorderly and bedraggled.

The cottage garden that surrounded the part of the house where Maisie and Pender lived together always seemed to

Dove to be incongruous but she pursued her policy of non-interference, drawing in silence the contrast of the bright, crowded planting with what she perceived as the serenity of her own green and restrained vistas. It was Pender who tended the garden, saving seed and making what he called 'swops' with his friends, taking slips and cuttings wherever he thought he would be unobserved, ingenuous at the surprise he encountered when some stolen treasure grew almost by default in one of his beds. Pender's talent for gardening, discovered late, now gave him the greatest pleasure in a life of small reversals.

Dove unlocked the door and went straight to her mother's kitchen, where she plugged in the kettle, removing plates and glasses from Pender's previous night's supper to the sink. He had left the cheese uncovered and the edges were already hard. Dove covered it with clingfilm, ignoring warnings on the box about contact with dairy foods, and put it into the little fridge, taking out an open carton of milk which she sniffed before pouring herself a mug of tea. Maisie preferred tea to be served in a cup and Dove carried both their drinks through to her mother, passing Pender's room and the open door of the sitting room on the way. She could see newspapers in an untidy bundle on the floor and smell stale air which she knew emanated from ashtrays which would be full to overflowing with Pender's dog-ends.

Dove put the cup and saucer on Maisie's night table, next to the copper tin of Rich Tea biscuits, and kissed her mother's cheek before drawing back the curtains at the window. They were old yellow velvet, faded to the colour of dying spring primroses where the sun had bleached the folds and Dove loved to run her hand over their familiar softness.

'I shall need a jigsaw, now that the weather's not so warm.' Maisie had been lying awake for an hour and her conversation with Dove proceeded without a break from the point she had reached in her own thoughts.

Dove was used to it and answered quite naturally, 'I'll look for one when I go out later to collect your crochet cotton – did I tell you that Beckerlegs 'phoned to say that it's in?'

'You did. But, Dove darling, listen a minute: I don't want flowers, tulips especially; nor harbour scenes or cottages with roses and a duck pond. You're so *good* at choosing puzzles but sometimes I do just wonder if I might have done them before.'

Dove Courtney smiled at her mother, thinking of the pile of jigsaw puzzles kept in the old toy cupboard, which she alternated with the ones she bought in charity shops and the occasional, brand new one which her daughters gave their grandmother on her birthday. Maisie always recognised the new ones, for a while at least, and it was some time before they could join the collection in the cupboard.

'Is there anything else you need before I go?' Dove looked around her mother's comfortable room. At the beginning of the day Maisie was nervous of falling and stayed in bed until Dove came to see her each morning. Each day, while Dove made the bed and opened the windows to air the room, Maisie washed herself in the bathroom which had been specially adapted for her in what had been a scullery at the back of the house.

Now Maisie looked at her daughter with a child's expression on her face. 'Is the bed all right?'

'Of course it's all right, I do wish you wouldn't worry so, I've got a perfectly good washing machine and it's no trouble at all to me.'

'I know that, and I know that you don't mind, but *I* mind. You have enough to do without me giving you extra work.'

Maisie slippered unsteadily towards the bathroom and

Dove returned to the vase of chrysanthemums which stood on a small table under the window. While she had been drawing the curtains Dove had identified them as the source of the sour, cloying smell in the bedroom. Now she took the decomposing flowers into the kitchen, pushing them into an already full plastic bag of rubbish which she would drop into the dustbin on her way round to her own door.

'If there's nothing else, I'll go then. Are you coming across at lunchtime? I could make a junket and get some of that nice ham.'

'No, darling. It's bridge here this afternoon, Enid and Girlie are coming.' Maisie hesitated, made up her mind, then took a letter out of the pocket of her dressing gown. 'This arrived yesterday.' She handed the letter to Dove, seeming to be reluctant to relinquish it. 'Your brother and his child bride are proposing to visit.'

'Oh, Mother, why didn't you tell me before? When are they coming?'

'Next week.' Maisie's reply was deliberately offhand and she said no more, but watched silently as Dove read Lawry's letter.

Dear old Dove's always so busy that I thought we could stay with you and Uncle Pen. We'd be no trouble, forage for ourselves, take you out for meals, etc. Will you let me know?

Dove looked at her mother. She had been trying to read the letter without her glasses and had to hold it as far away from her as her arm would stretch.

'What does he mean, "We'd be no trouble"? It would be nothing but trouble if they stayed here. There are no spare beds and as you've only got the microwave and the kettle they'd be in and out to us at the house the whole time – and just think how Pen would hate to share the bathroom with them. No, of course they can't stay here: you must tell him at once, Mother, and tell him at the same time that I'll put them up.' She added to herself, 'Probably what he was fishing for, anyway.'

Maisie took the letter back before Dove had a chance to read the piece in a different handwriting which appeared after Lawry's signature. Obviously from the child bride, Dove thought, and would have liked to know what she had written. There was a photograph in the envelope and Maisie silently handed this to Dove. It showed Lawry, smiling and sunburned, with his arm around a young woman with frazzled blonde hair and bright, skimpy clothes. There were several other people grouped around a table but it was difficult to see them clearly as it was a poor photograph. It seemed to have been taken indoors, in a bar perhaps, and looked almost varnished, several of the group with disturbing red eyes.

'She's certainly got a rush of teeth to her head,' Maisie said. 'Smile like Red Rum.'

Dove looked carefully at her brother's companion. 'She's,' Dove began. 'Well, she's . . .'

'Common.'

'Mother!'

'And too young. Much too young. *Why* is he such a fool?'

Dove handed back the picture. 'Fool or not, she's his wife and we must try to make her welcome. After all, they won't be here for long so we'll just have to make the best of it.' She looked sideways at Maisie. 'You will behave, won't you Mother?'

Maisie returned the banal little picture to the envelope without giving it another look and without answering Dove's anxious question.

As she walked the few yards back to the main house Dove thought about her brother and reluctantly acknowledged the usual irritation at the way in which they all accepted his haplessness. Had he really not intended to warn her that he and his wife were coming to stay and did he not understand at all his mother's situation?

She slipped off her damp shoes inside the back door, smelled burned toast and realised that Lewis must be down and making his own breakfast. He looked up as Dove came into the kitchen, from long experience seeing at once that she had something on her mind. 'Sorry about all the smoke, the bread got jammed again. I'll fix it later on.'

'You've been saying that for weeks, why don't we just buy a new toaster? I'll pick one up when I go into town if you like.'

Lewis opened several cupboard doors looking for cereal, and smiled at Dove as she found and placed on the table muesli, milk, a bowl and a spoon. He took several mouthfuls before he spoke again. 'Maisie all right this morning?'

'Maisie's fine.' Dove poured herself another, stronger, mug of tea and stood leaning against the sink, looking out at the damp garden, trees just outlined in the misty air. 'I'm not.'

'I can see that. Want to tell me what's the matter?'

'Lawry, and what my mother will refer to as the child bride, are coming to stay next week and, of course, he hasn't bothered to let me know. He actually asked Maisie if they could stay next door with her and Pen.'

'What's wrong with that?'

'Do be sensible, Lewis. There isn't room for them over there so they'll have to come here.'

'And?'

'And, oh I don't know. I feel aggrieved with him, springing a new wife on us as he has without any hint that there was even anyone in the offing. It's so typical of Lawry and I was fond of Virginia; I can't just pretend that she didn't exist.'

'You don't have to, do you? Anyway, it's hardly likely

that he'll want to talk about her in front of a new wife, is it? Give the child bride a chance, Dove. Don't frighten her, will you?'

'Would I do that?' Dove thought of her own, unanswered, warning to her mother.

'Oh yes! And we should stop calling her that or we'll come out with it to her face. Shall I have another try at some toast?'

Dove shook her head. 'Not for me, I must get going. See you at lunchtime. Oh, and Lewis, could you speak to Pen if you've got five minutes?'

'If I could speak to your uncle in five minutes, believe me I would, but it'll take all bloody morning, you know what he's like.'

'Tell him you've got choir practice in half an hour or something. Please, Lewis.'

Lewis got up from the table and put his arms around Dove. He had a very characteristic smell, spicy, almost foreign, and when they had first met it used to intoxicate her. Just lately she had found it not to her liking. 'For you, cariad, anything. I'll take him to The Tinners'.' Lewis kissed the back of Dove's neck and she pulled away, smoothing her hair upwards into the chignon she had recently taken to wearing.

'The Tinners' Arms is probably what it's all about. I expect he owes them money again.'

'Easily sorted then.'

'You are a kind man, Lewis.' Dove stopped at the kitchen door as if she were going to say something more but instead took her basket off the hook and went through to the front of the house to put on her macintosh.

Dove stood by the railings on the promenade shivering a little. She longed for the cool morning air to scour from her skin the smell of Lewis's body; the wind to blow her hair free of their shared, middle-aged dependence.

She watched the grey water receding, leaving banks of wet sand isolated like islands, tiny microcosms with only a solitary gull as population. Each wave left behind slippery, olive-brown seaweed that was piled, abandoned by the water, until the next high tide should reclaim it. It smelled of decay and salt and every other morning that Dove Courtney had leaned on the green railings which separated the promenade from the beach.

As a child she had watched just as she did now, waiting for pools to appear at the base of the rocks, where later she and Lawry would fish for the small, brown shrimps which they were never allowed to eat. Sometimes it was a crab or a dying fish that they caught and which they were made to empty from their painted tin buckets before they went home. Occasionally they found brittle white cuttlefish which they jammed through the bars of the cage of Winston, their grandmother's canary. Sometimes it was seagulls' feathers which, if they were clean, they painted and stuck onto bands of brown paper which were growing slowly into Indian headdresses. Dove had especially prized the shells which looked to her like babies' fingernails and which she wrapped in her handkerchief for safekeeping. By the time she remembered and retrieved them they were nearly always crushed into splintered, pearly pieces and had to be thrown away, the grit and sand, which was all that was left of their fragility, shaken from her pocket.

While Dove had looked for mermaids' purses, Lawry hunted for coins in the shingle under the wall where people liked to sit with their back against the sun-warmed stone, out of the wind. Anything he found he kept and he laid his treasures in a row on his bedroom windowsill, a surprising number of discoloured sixpences and threepenny bits among the large, brown pennies. Once there had been half-a-crown and this he had shared with Dove, as he had always shared anything of value with her: the collapse of his business; the failure of his first marriage; his mystifying inability to be happy for more than a short time – all these he shared with Dove, and now he was bringing her his new wife and he expected Dove to share her home with someone she regarded almost as a usurper; kind, untidy Virginia replaced by a girl scarcely older than Dove's own daughters.

It was unfair to think like that and Dove knew it and she knew, too, that it was with Lawry that she was annoyed, not the unknown woman he had married so soon after meeting her on a singles holiday in the south of France.

The problem of her disaffection for Lewis was more troubling to Dove, who accepted that her feelings for him had changed subtly over the years, but in a way which she accepted, understood, to be quite usual in a long marriage. They had always been comfortable together, Dove well aware that she had demanded far more from the marriage than Lewis had ever done.

He had no close family, no ties, no allegiance to anything except to Dove, their daughters and the Welsh Rugby Union. He sang with the local male voice choir and his beautiful baritone voice moved Dove much more than his physical presence had for a long time. In spite of her present uncertainties, Dove still thought that Lewis Courtney was one of the handsomest men she had ever seen. He had thick, black hair which even now at fifty-two showed hardly any grey; and curious, triangular shaped eyes which turned darker than ever with emotion. A black Welshman with golden, almost Mediterranean skin, and a nose as high bridged and curved as a parrot's beak.

Dove, who had always been attracted to men with big noses, had been captivated by Lewis as soon as they met and had overlooked the fact that he was of only medium height and rather broad and stocky. She had always imagined herself married to a man with wavy, pale hair who had narrow legs and fingers and that their sons would be blond and take after their father.

Lewis and Dove's three daughters were like their father, small and dark and beautiful, but only Jossy the youngest, had his tolerant, pragmatic temperament and soon now Jossy would be leaving home to go to university and Dove and Lewis would be on their own in the house which had been filled by their family for thirty years.

They would not be alone, of course; there were Maisie and Pender just on the other side of the dividing wall and they were taking up more and more of Dove's time. She did wonder, though, if her feelings towards Lewis which were causing her so much anxiety, were only temporary, the result of a natural reluctance to part with her last child, or whether something in their relationship had changed in a way she had yet to understand.

While Dove had been watching the tide go out, a rainstorm had been building over the sea. Seagulls' wings made a glistening silver squadron as they skimmed and turned low over the water, and Dove felt the rush of cold air that precedes rain. The buildings around the harbour looked close enough to touch against a backdrop of clouds coloured like hammered pewter, streaking grey on the horizon where rain was already falling over the Mount.

Dove shivered again and walked back to her car, driving to a quiet road where she knew that she could park for long enough to do her shopping. It wasn't too difficult to find a place now that most of the visitors had gone home but the traffic wardens never relaxed their vigilance and Dove felt her usual stab of annoyance that residents of the town should be treated in the same way as holiday makers.

Here, away from the main streets, grey walls were topped by faded valerian and trails of toadflax which would bloom sturdily for a few months yet, purple flowers like miniature snapdragons bright against heart-shaped leaves which softened and clothed the stones. There was bitter green stonecrop and still a few small scabious which must have grown from seed blown inland from the cliffs, hairy flowers paler mauve than the toadflax. Dove loved these impromptu gardens almost more than her own green, enclosed wilderness which never seemed to look exactly as she retained it in her mind, taking her by surprise each time that she returned to it.

The gardens which surrounded Rejerrah could have been described as colourless but Dove found it a challenge to balance green against green, shape and outline more important to her than brightness or variety. There was colour from azaleas and rhododendrons in the early part of the year; philadelphus shone into June, and hydrangeas and fuschias grew almost unconstrained wherever they had found a foothold. It was the absence of flower beds which made the garden unusual; shrubs and stands of grass and bamboo forming a pattern with the trees which Dove's grandfather had planted and which were now fully grown and glorious.

A medlar tree grew on either side of a pergola and the orange globes of a passion fruit which had colonised the wooden support nestled in the bushy leaves like Christmas lights turned on too early. There was a grove of walnut trees and two black mulberries, and agaves in a group which reminded Dove of Degas' little dancers in ragged, yellowing tutus. Dove's favourite of the garden's trees was a Robinia, which had been planted by her grandfather to stabilise the bottom of an embankment and which was now almost at its full height. It was here that Dove had placed a wooden bench and table and where she sat to write letters and to make lists of things to be remembered. By autumn the tassels of white flowers which brightened the early summer had turned to hard, dark pods. When Dove's daughters had been small they had searched in the long grass to find pods fallen from the tree to use in their games of shop or cooking, and in the tree's shade secrets had been traded, hearts broken, trysts contracted.

There was little in the garden that could be spoiled by children's games and as tricycles and a sandpit gave way to tennis and a sort of croquet, the garden continued to grow lush and green. In dry years the grass was scorched but always, mysteriously, grew again from seemingly dead roots, and in the years when it rained, too much clover and moss dappled the ground. No matter how hot it was, there was always shade in the garden and under the trees; in the secret green shadows there seemed to be a dampness which was never entirely diffused. There were hidden places in the gardens of Rejerrah; covert, leafy rooms where life could be lived, clandestine and concealed.

Dove and Lewis's first child had been conceived in one of these arcane, dusky arbours, on a night when the moon had silvered the ground and moths had shared the magic on silent, powdery wings. When the baby was born, Lewis had looked at her in silence for a long time. He had been hoping for a prop forward, as a child might have preferred a puppy, but he had turned to Dove and smiled his gratitude.

'We should call her after the Goddess of the Moon – what do you think of Diana?'

Dove, remembering the shadowy pattern of leaves thrown over both of them by moonlight as bright as day and the sweet, night-time smell of the syringa bushes, had agreed at once and it became a secret they shared, their happiness spreading like a protective veil over their daughter.

Lewis's full-back was born four years later and called Bethan after his mother; Jossy being his last try for a scrum half six years after that. Never once did he allow any disappointment to cloud Dove's contentment as each daughter was born, and if Dove ever allowed herself to guess at his feelings she kept her own counsel, confiding only in Maisie.

Maisie's brother could have been Lewis's ally in that household of women but Pender Woodvine was a man unsuited to the demands of male fellowship. He had left Oxford at twenty-one and he had drifted for over fifty years; impermanently employed, intermittently unsuitably attached and always, overridingly, short of money. He seemed not to be able to grasp the correlation between work and solvency and said that he preferred not to fill his brain with useless information; information, which he implied, could very well impede him in the acceptance of any particular situation towards which he might find himself propelled.

It was true that he had worked for Maisie's husband, Eddie Eustace, for a few years, making his job as book-keeper sound as onerous as that assigned to St Peter, but when Eddie Eustace had joined the navy in 1940, it was not Pender but Maisie who had taken over the running of the business. She had sent Lawry and Dove to live with her parents at Rejerrah and had persuaded Pender, who had been classed as unfit for military service, to work hard for the first time in his life. Maisie refused to pay him unless she judged that he had earned his wages and Pender, patriotism of a sort acting as a spur to his conscience, threw himself into keeping track of the accounts and dockets and emissions from various war ministries.

Eustace and Son, Seed and Agricultural Merchants, had a brief flourishing under Maisie and Pender's care, neither totally scrupulous in their business methods but both successful in persuading debtors to find the money to settle outstanding accounts and pursuing slightly questionable ways of obtaining scarce materials.

Eddie Eustace, meanwhile, was on a minesweeper, away

for months at a time. It was in May 1944 while clearing channels in preparation for D-Day that a mine, unseen and implacable, had blown apart his ship and everyone in her. Maisie, widowed at thirty, had scarcely faltered. Four years apart, doing a man's work with only Pender to rely on, had altered her so that it was almost as if she had heard only of the death of a good friend, not of a husband whom she had believed herself to love.

Dove and Lawry, secure and happy at Rejerrah with their Woodvine grandparents, had been hardly more affected by their father's death. Dove remembered him only as a smell of tobacco; rough, dark material scratching her bare arms and legs, and a silence when he had gone. Lawry, at six, had pictures still vivid enough of a man with big hands who lit the candles on his birthday cake and who had made him sit still for a long time while his new baby sister was arranged on a cushion at his side on a wide, squashy sofa from which he couldn't escape. Big hands, covered in golden hairs which reminded Lawry of his teddy bear, had stretched the little boy's arm around the cushion and he had been told to smile at the baby.

Maisie still had the photograph. It showed a bewildered two year old in a smocked romper suit and the softest ankle strap shoes looking with distaste and reluctance at a lace dress from which protruded a large, round face which, even then, seemed to be set in an expression of determination. Someone had hand coloured the portrait and both children had the incongruous eyebrows and red lips of a currently popular film star.

The box containing the new toaster was too big to fit into any of Dove's shopping bags so she had to balance it uncomfortably on her left arm, her right hand clutching both a basket and a plastic bag. By the time she reached her car the handles of the carrier had stretched into a thin, biting string which had turned her fingers blue. Dove put it down carefully and flexed her fingers before unlocking the boot and carefully stacking everything inside; bottles upright, eggs flat and all wedged tightly so that no sudden movement should dislodge them.

The awkwardness of carrying too much at once had made Dove's back ache and she slid into the driving seat, glad to have finished and to be on her way home. She had just started the car when she remembered Maisie's crochet cotton, which she had promised to collect from Beckerlegs in Market Jew Street. Just for a moment Dove wondered if she should leave it but thinking of Maisie's disappointment and lack of reproach, which was harder to bear than any reprimand, she got out of the car, turned into the road she had just struggled along and walked back down the narrow street, pressing herself against the window of an empty, dusty butcher's shop as a van crept down the middle of the road, inches to spare between its tarpaulin covered sides and the fronts of the houses left unprotected by the absence of a pavement. A car was parked on the corner blocking the exit and the driver of the van stopped: he seemed unfazed and smiled at Dove before slowly reversing back the way he had just come. Dove followed him, retreat cut off, self-consciously aware of being watched, and as he turned into the market square the driver turned and waved at her.

Normally it would have cheered her but today she found his insouciance irritating and hurried to Beckerlegs, her face closed against further intrusion. Dove asked for the cotton, polite but unforthcoming to enquiries after Maisie.

'I expect you're all looking forward to meeting the new Mrs Eustace drec'ly.' The elder Miss Beckerleg was placing the spools of thread individually into a paper bag, shifting and adjusting each one to lie neatly against its neighbour. Dove wanted to snatch the bag from the grey, wrinkled hands and to flee back to her car, to Rejerrah and its enclosing green privacy.

She gave a forced apology for a smile and said nothing, unjustifiably angry that news of Lawry's arrival should already be a matter of gossip and that Miss Beckerleg's faded sherry eyes which were watching her over spectacles that had slipped down her greasy nose, saw so much which Dove would prefer to conceal.

'Sixteen pounds please, Mrs Courtney. Oh, sorry my dear, we don't take credit cards – you must have forgotten.'

Dove sighed and opened her purse, taking out her last £20 note. Now she would have to go to the bank before she could go home and it seemed suddenly almost too much to expect of her.

'Are you all right, Mrs Courtney? You don't look too clever this morning.' Miss Beckerleg put four coins into Dove's hand, holding it from underneath with her own free hand as if it needed support. 'I expect you could do with a holiday.' Dove withdrew her hand quickly from Miss Beckerleg's unwelcome embrace. 'One of those coach tours you go on. On your own,' Miss Beckerleg added, her voice guileless, spite only in her eyes.

'Thank you, Miss Beckerleg, I'm quite well but if I do go on holiday I'm sure that you'll be the first to know.' The chiming bells which hung on the back of the shop door to alert the Misses Beckerleg to customers, swung and tinkled as Dove slammed it behind her. Cissy Beckerleg wrote the transaction into her cash book, pleased with the reaction she had provoked. Maisie Eustace's daughter was not like her mother, thought Cissy, too opinionated by half. Cissy remembered her own niece, Gracie's daughter, who looked so like Dove, but Dove copied by an artist of little skill, the features blunter and coarse in a way that blurred the resemblance to all but those who knew the truth.

The house was quiet when Dove let herself in, making

several journeys to the car for her bags and baskets. She didn't think that she would need to go out again and when she had finished unloading her shopping she drove the car into the garage, noticing that Enid Glazzard's old but shiny Triumph was already standing outside Maisie's door.

Dove decided that the delivery of her mother's prescription and embroidery cotton could wait until her evening visit and was relieved to see that Lewis' Rover was not in its accustomed place, which meant that she could read her *Daily Mail*, untouched that morning in her rush to get out, and eat in peace the prawn and mayonnaise sandwich which she had bought herself in town. It was a small indulgence but one over which Dove sometimes felt uneasy as if such prodigality might lead her to further excesses over which she no longer had control, and she ate the sandwich quickly, hiding its stiff plastic wrapper under rubbish already in the dustbin.

The garage in which Dove had left her car was a separate building from the house, a flight of outside steps leading to a small flat over the open space below. It had once been stabling for the horses belonging to the sporting parson who had lived in Rejerrah when it was new, and it stood along the second side of the square formed by the house and its enclosing wall. From the road this wall concealed the house, four hexagonal chimneys and the stab of scarlet Virginia Creeper in the autumn the only sign to passers-by that a substantial building lay hidden, tantalisingly just out of sight. There was a pair of gates as high as the wall; they often stood open, privacy uncompromised as the curve of the drive and a thicket of rhododendrons and arbutus trees shielded the life lived at Rejerrah from the inquisitive.

When Dove had finished her surreptitious sandwich, she plugged in the kettle to make tea and went to fetch a notepad and pen from their appointed place on a corner of the dresser. Dove selected a pen with care from a bunch arranged like truncated flowers in a cracked and leaky mug which one of the children had given her and which she found impossible to throw away. She chose a mauve pen, not recognising it and wondering where it had come from, before settling down at the table. Before she could start, the kettle turned itself off and she rose again with a sigh to make the tea before once more sitting down and opening the notebook.

Lawry and . . ., she wrote and stopped, realising that she didn't know the name of her brother's new wife. She tried again. *Lawry and T.Ch.B's. visit.* Dove underlined these words and started to make her list.

1. *Clean room.*
2. *Make up bed. ?Spare pillows.*
3. *Menus for 2 weeks.*
4. *Make shopping list.*
5. *Do shopping MONDAY. ?Flowers.*
6. *Maisie – hair? If yes, make appointment.*
7. *Book holiday.*

Dove looked at this last item as if it had appeared on the page in front of her by some agency other than her own hand and knew that it was the one thing that she actually wanted to do. She crossed it out, turned to a fresh page and started a new list. This one was all the meals that she imagined a family of seven would eat in two weeks, and when she had done that, she started to write down ingredients and to make a detailed shopping list.

Dove enjoyed making lists; it gave her a temporary feeling of control over events which she felt might otherwise engulf her. She heard Lewis' car returning but scarcely looked up as he came into the kitchen.

'Spoke to Pender for you.'

'Um-mh?'

'Any tea left?'

'Probably.' Dove wrote down, *Selection of cheeses*. 'What did you say?'

'I said that I've spoken to Pen.'

'And?'

'Not money this time.' Lewis had poured himself a mug of lukewarm tea and he sat down opposite Dove, the length of the kitchen table between them. Dove put down her mauve pen and looked at Lewis, impatience at being interrupted overlaid by curiosity. Lewis smiled at her, deliberately provocative, but Dove waited and eventually he said, 'He thinks he's in love.'

'Oh, for God's sake, he's seventy-five, who'd have him?'

'That, apparently, is the trouble. Unrequited love.'

'Do you really expect me to take such nonsense seriously?'

'Oh come on Dove, don't be too hard on him, he's really in a bit of a state about it.' Lewis turned his mug round and round in his hands, looking at the scum cooling on top of his tea. 'Won't last, of course, but we ought to try to give him a bit of sympathy, poor old sod.'

'Poor is right; old is right; and sod is most certainly right. Whoever is she, Lewis? I thought he was carrying a still flickering torch for Girlie Eustace.'

'Of course he is, but that's been going on for so long that it's just part of his life: this is different and – oh Lord – you're going to love this.' Lewis tipped his chair back on two legs in the way that had irritated Dove so much when the girls used to do it. He looked at her, mischief in his triangular eyes. 'It's that little blonde woman, Anita I think she's called, who joined the Yacht Club this summer.'

'Not the one like a nodding dog?'

Lewis snapped the chair back and Dove pictured Anita, eager and overdressed, her head tick-tocking acknowledgement of every word spoken to her as if agitated by some hidden compulsion to emphasise her agreement. She saw the pearly pink mouth and the unfashionable, shimmery blue eyeshadow and hair bleached almost to the colour of a dandelion clock, but straight and becoming around a jawline not yet beginning to sag. Suddenly Dove felt old and tired; she put down her pen and closed the notebook.

'I don't understand what's happening to the men in this family,' she said. 'Lawry married to a girl whose name we don't even know but who looks totally unsuitable; and now Pender, randy old goat, imagining himself in love with that silly little woman.' Dove closed her eyes and then opened them to find Lewis watching her, his expression one she was not able immediately to interpret. 'I'm pretty sick of it all, actually, because I know who they'll come to to pick up the pieces when it's tears before bedtime.'

'Why should it come to tears? Lawry's responsible enough to know what he's doing, and . . .'

'. . . Lawry will never be responsible enough to know what he's doing,' Dove interrupted Lewis, her voice full of accumulated vexation.

'And,' Lewis continued, using the emphasis which his daughters recognised as the one which meant that they had gone too far. 'And,' he went on, 'Pen is entitled to fall in love whenever and with whomsoever he pleases. And what's more,' Lewis said, 'I hope I shall still be able to feel enough to fall in love when I'm his age – and if it's with someone unsuitable, all the better.'

There was silence in the kitchen, Dove looking at the cover of her notebook on which was scrawled a telephone number which meant nothing to her. She concentrated on the figures because she didn't want to look at Lewis, unable to understand his ferocity; apprehensive that someone on whom she relied so totally for support seemed suddenly unwilling even to pretend to understand how she felt.

Dove got up and went, notebook in hand, to check

through her linen cupboard; to choose from the piles of neatly ironed sheets and duvet covers those she thought would be most suitable for her visitors. There was no need for them to suffer just because Lewis was being so unreasonable.

2

Enid Glazzard was preparing lunch in Maisie's little kitchen. She had brought a bowl of Coronation Chicken with her, the meat already cut into small cubes so that Girlie would be able to feed herself without too much help.

Pender had wandered into the kitchen, kissed Enid on the cheek, left a glass of sherry on the draining board, and wandered out again. Enid supposed that he was talking to Maisie and Girlie and wondered if the chicken would stretch to four, but she heard the front door close and knew that he had gone out.

She put the empty bowl into the sink and picked up the glass Pender had left for her. Good sherry, not too sweet, just as she liked it. Enid wondered if Pender's new friend drank sherry but she knew instinctively that she did not. She had noticed that younger women drank white wine or mineral water, sherry was only for the middle aged. The one good thing arising from Girlie's inability to move around unaided, Enid thought, was that every-one who mattered came to see her, and Enid, always present, solicitous and observant, heard all there was to hear.

She had known about Pender Woodvine's latest infat-uation almost as soon as Maisie had, and certainly long before Lewis had told Dove about it. It was a matter of passing interest to her, more for the diversion it would afford Girlie than for any real concern that Enid had for Pender Woodvine's welfare. Girlie's wellbeing was the pivot on which their life together turned and Enid's solicitude was only for her friend: Pender she regarded as no more than an amusing but ultimately negligible trespasser, the jester who attended court only on commission.

In disregarding the attachment which existed between Girlie Eustace and Pender Woodvine, by diminishing to a diversion their true affection, Enid Glazzard did them a disservice. Their attachment was one which allowed Girlie to retain independence of mind, physical freedom reduced to memory only, since her stroke.

It was Pender's elder brother Grenfell to whom Girlie had been engaged but Grenfell Woodvine, older, handsomer and more earnest than Pender, had been killed in the Blitz in the second year of the war. Neither Girlie nor his family ever knew just why he had been in London on that particular night and Girlie had waited, fretting and displeased, not to hear from him.

A man who walked upright and impenetrable like a soldier had travelled to Cornwall to talk to the Woodvines but it was Verena, Grenfell's mother, who had deflected her own grief until she had explained to Girlie that she must make plans for her future that no longer included marriage to Grenfell: Grenfell was dead, buried under the remains of a building in Whitehall whose function would be for ever concealed.

Girlie had looked at Verena Woodvine, her blue eyes hurt and uncomprehending as if Grenfell's dying was somehow personal, a snub, a slight to her suitability as his future wife. For a long time Girlie seemed unable to comprehend the finality of Grenfell's death and went about as usual in her chosen war work of organising a canteen for the servicemen who passed through Penalverne, where her figure and blonde hair soon earned her the nickname of Cornwall's Betty Grable.

A part of Verena died with her elder son and many times she wished that she could learn to live like Girlie, grief compartmentalised, veiled and private, for only Verena knew how Girlie suffered. Where others perceived shallowness and frivolity, Verena saw the strength of Girlie's courage. Girlie Eustace never married, laughingly saying that her heart had been broken once – and only those who knew her well heard the bitter truth in what she said. When Girlie's brother, Eddie Eustace, had married Grenfell's sister, Maisie, she had become close once more to the Woodvines and Maisie and Pender always thought of Girlie as their sister-in-law and a member of the family as surely as if Grenfell had married her.

At seventy-two, Girlie Eustace was still as charming and full of allure as she had been at eighteen, her now slightly lopsided face adding character to features which seemed to have been smoothed by her stroke and returned to the delicacy of those of a young woman. No one meeting Girlie for the first time thought how lovely she must once have been but only what a pretty woman she was.

Pender had been in love with her from the first time that Grenfell had brought her home, more suitably near her age than his older brother, but knowing even then that he had no chance with her. Girlie's tact and kindness had always held his interest in check but over the years small incursions, private generosities, shared joy, had slipped almost unseen through cracks in her reserve, their devotion to one another increasing as the years passed.

There had been many suitors for Girlie's hand and she enjoyed the attentions of a slightly old-fashioned kind with which she was surrounded by the men who were attracted to her. She watched with tolerance and sympathetic distress as her friends brought up children and became reluctantly assimilated into wider, complicated families of half and step relationships as those children married and remarried. She was, Girlie thought, fortunate not to lose grandchildren to a foreign country with a vengeful daughter-in-law or to experience the difficulty of having to give every indication of impartiality towards unknown, unlovely children to ease the beginning of a new marriage, as she had seen close friends struggling to do.

Girlie liked being alone, something not understood by those who dismissed her as a woman incapable of deep thought. Protected by hair more golden now than at twenty, and the glamorous, rather outdated manner of a 1940s' film star, Girlie Eustace possessed the strength of character which enabled her to bear with such uncomplaining graciousness the indignities forced on her by illness. Her speech was hardly affected and, guarded and attended by Enid Glazzard, Girlie continued her life of coffee mornings and bridge parties, as vivacious and entertaining as she had always been.

Enid Glazzard, disregarding her own appearance both from lack of interest and pressure of time, had spent a lifetime teaching children to ride, and now she groomed and beautified Girlie as if she were being prepared for a show. Enid's interest in cosmetics and fashion had always been minimal but, in looking after Girlie, something not quite suppressed in her nature was given unexpected access and the two women lived together with every indication of harmony.

Enid had certainly never envisaged a life among soft, warm surroundings where every comfort was anticipated and provided for as a matter of course; where food was enjoyed and a subject for discussion; time spent with friends a pleasure for which one planned. Any money Enid had was spent, not on decorations or in buying new furnishings, but on patching and mending the fabric of her house; replacing any household item a serious undertaking ventured upon only in dire necessity, and sometimes not even then. People who knew her only a little saw her big house, the horses, heard her loud, confident voice and thought her eccentric, not understanding at all that Enid Glazzard had made a virtue of poverty and hardly noticed her own discomfort any more.

The Glazzard School of Riding had flourished for a while but as more and more children began to be able to afford to buy their own ponies Enid had been reduced to taking in horses at livery and slowly decay and unintentional neglect had crept almost unnoticed over her fields and stables. Enid's knowledge of horses kept her in demand at the Pony Club and as a judge at gymkhanas, her old blue dress and heavy, laced-up shoes unvarying from one summer to the next.

Her parents' house, too big, too empty and much too cold, would have been a burden to Enid had she been less stalwart. With her lurcher, Sandy, she lived in the kitchen, cutting wood when she couldn't afford coke to burn in the stove, cooking only when, occasionally, she felt that she really needed a hot meal. She still slept upstairs but was considering the feasibility of bringing her bed down to the morning room. It was the necessity of using the bathroom that kept her from making this change as the downstairs lavatory was at the end of an unlit corridor and too hazardous an expedition even for Enid to undertake willingly any more at night with only a torch to light the way. She hadn't minded it when she was younger but any feeling of adventure had been dissipated when she had tripped over an uneven flagstone and turned her ankle badly enough to hamper her everyday activities.

Enid was the same age as her friend Girlie Eustace, but looked ten years older; weatherbeaten where Girlie was cosseted, dressed always in worn cords and boots where Girlie's silk shirts and expensive shoes drew attention everywhere to her neat figure and tiny feet. Enid's obstinacy and determination to manage on her own had aged her as surely as Girlie's self-indulgence had been a protection from the derogation of age.

They had been at school together, drifting apart for a while during the war but, in a town like Penalverne loyalties were strong and although their lives were so different, each liked the other and was glad to meet now and again to exchange news, small in Enid's case; to be aware of the wellbeing of the other.

When Girlie had a stroke two weeks before her seventieth birthday her party was cancelled, her friends informed and Enid Glazzard was among the first of those who went to visit her. Girlie sat in a chair beside the bed, her hair combed but in need of its usual highlight and set, looking somehow diminished, and it hurt Enid to see her so. She had gone home and sat in her own bleak, not very clean kitchen and thought for a long time.

There were half a dozen horses in the paddock – no need to get rid of them at once – only a few pupils, who would probably cheerfully transfer to a new school, and a house quietly crumbling around her. Enid's thoughts were not altogether altruistic: years of living without having to consider anyone else's welfare before her own had not made solicitude for others something in which she readily engaged, but she had had an offer to buy her house and land for development and Enid had been tempted.

It was a long time since Enid's thoughts had strayed from the prosaic – the necessity of affording feed for the animals, the ability to pay the plumber when the pipes had burst and flooded the bathroom at the end of the previous winter – but slowly she came to understand that Girlie's gaiety was something more than the manifestation of the easy life of a pampered woman. Enid recognised Girlie's spirit as an antidote to the grievousness of life, her blitheness as evidence of something more than the unwavering slog into which her own life had degenerated.

Enid was wondering how to resolve her thoughts into action when Pender Woodvine came to see her; Pender had friends everywhere and he had heard of the offer to buy Enid's house. He allowed her to understand this as he sat, good manners overriding fastidiousness, on one of her kitchen chairs, lately vacated by Sandy the lurcher who had patches of mange showing through his coat and who now sat at Pender's feet, eyes full of the knowledge of his unwholesomeness to a man who disliked dogs. But Pender was a kind man and felt uneasy under Sandy's gaze so he put out his hand and touched him lightly on the head where there seemed to be a full complement of hair. 'How did you find Girlie?' Pender accepted a mug of tea from Enid, trying not to dwell on the tidemark on the inside of the china, drinking at an odd angle to avoid the brown stain on the rim.

'Better than I feared, not as good as I hoped – bit seedy, really.' Enid held her mug in both hands, looking at Pender. Suddenly she lifted the mug to her mouth and drank all of its contents in one go. 'What's she going to do when she goes home, d'you suppose? Can't manage on her own, can she?'

Pender abandoned the pretence of drinking from the unsavoury mug and put it down on the kitchen table. 'No,' he said. 'No, she won't be able to manage without a bit of help.'

'Lucky she can still talk reasonably well.'

'Very lucky.' Pender watched as Enid prised the lid off a tin of shortbread left over from Christmas.

'Biccy?' Pender shook his head and Enid, after tasting one of the biscuits herself, emptied the rest of the tin onto the floor. The mangy dog swooped on this bounty, chasing crumbs and licking the floor clean, dark pathways of saliva criss crossing the stone floor.

Pender watched this pantomime in silence and Enid suddenly laughed and said, 'Afraid living on one's own leads to bad habits, you forget the niceties. Girlie would never chuck crumbs onto the floor, would she?'

'Never.'

'And you're afraid that if I were persuaded to go and stay with her for a while, I should bring my uncivilised behaviour into her life.'

Pender caught unawares by Enid's intuition looked nearly as uncomfortable as a man used to inhabiting the unaccommodating corners of life had the right to do. He wondered how much more of his mind was open to her.

Enid watched him for a minute or two, unwilling to help him out of his difficulty. At last she said, 'Oh, come on Pen, we've known each other too long for any pretence between us. You know my circumstances, as you know everyone's. Oh yes you do, you old fraud.' Pender's attempt at denial was dismissed as Enid went on, 'I've been thinking along the same lines myself, can't say that I haven't.'

'And have you reached any conclusion?'

'Perhaps. More tea? Oh, you haven't finished the first one – something wrong with it?'

Pender stood up to cover the necessity of answering Enid's question and then, finding no reason not to, he sat down again. He felt uncomfortably hot and there was an undefinable smell in the kitchen which he hoped was attributable to Sandy. In any case, Enid had always unnerved him, used as he was to women of a more susceptible nature. Something in her vigorous self-reliance, the unbecoming hairnet and masculine clothes that she wore, suggested to Pender Woodvine that she found it easy to resist his, almost, unintentional charm. In her presence he became monosyllabic, allowing her no access to argument, to disparagement or ridicule. It was not that Pender disliked Enid; they had, as she said, known each other for a long time – but he was a little afraid of her.

Girlie Eustace seemed to be everything that Enid was not; amenable, appreciative and with every appearance of that reliant femininity which appealed to a man whose life had always been dependent upon the support of a woman. Enid gave no indication of needing a man to complement her life although Pender could remember a time when, as a young woman, her name had been linked with more than one married man and there had been a longer liaison with someone her father had regarded as unsuitable for marriage into the family. Perhaps he had been right, for in the end Enid's fiancé had proved unable to withstand the aloof indifference of the Glazzards and had married well and happily outside the tight little circle of old farming families. If Enid felt any lingering regret that she wasn't the mother of his six children she never allowed it to show. When he had left her Enid had opened the riding school, her father and brothers simply not aware that she was unhappy.

Pender knew most of this, Maisie filling in the details where his memory was hazy. He hadn't thought of it for years, until Enid's name kept insinuating itself into his mind when he was wondering how best to help Girlie Eustace. He knew Enid to be dependable, not squeamish, and unsentimentally kind – and he had heard that she was in very low water financially.

'There's one thing, Pen.' Pender withdrew his revolted gaze from Sandy who was now exploring between his hind legs with a large rough tongue. 'What about the dog? Can't possibly consider doing without him and I don't know that Girlie's flat is big enough for him, he's used to a lot of freedom.'

Pender looked at Enid, his face carefully neutral. 'Ummh, a *petit* problem I hadn't considered.' Neither of them

believed this: they were both well aware that behind Pender
Woodvine's façade of artful amiability was a mind both
astute and discerning. Enid knew very well that he would
have explored every possibility of a solution to the problem
of Girlie's welfare and in approaching Enid, Pender would
have examined and disposed of all the subtleties of her
position.

Enid waited, determined not to be forced into a solution
she would regret. At last Pender, pretending to have been
thinking about what Enid had said, looked at her, his
face full of sudden, practised resolution. 'How about me
taking Sandy? You could see him every day and there's
plenty of space for him to run about.' He looked at the
big, grey animal. 'Maisie won't mind, she's always rather
liked dogs.'

'It isn't Maisie who would need not to mind, it's Dove.
What would she think? It's her house, after all, and I
can't see you trailing around her precious garden with a
pooper-scooper and a plastic bag.'

'There's the field behind the house; no reason why he
should need to go into Dove's garden at all. Not without
an invitation anyway – bit like me and Maisie.'

'You'd really do that for Girlie?'

'I'd do anything for Girlie, including taking in your
damned dog but that, my dear, is strictly *entre nous*. I
shall tell people that I felt sorry for you having to sell
the farm and that I felt sorry for poor, homeless Sandy
and was prevailed upon, against my better judgement, to
give him succour.'

'If I can see him when I want and if I'm sure that you're
looking after him well enough, then I might seriously
consider your offer.'

'Good enough, Enid, I thought we'd see eye to eye. Now,
how about a proper drink? I stopped at the off-licence on
the way here for the monthly supplies so if you try to find

some clean glasses, I'll fetch the hooch.' Pender stood up, Sandy's eyes following him as he walked to the door.

Outside, the sky was skimmed with tiny, broken clouds, promise of good weather to come, and Pender stopped to watch a flock of birds flying inland for the night. He looked around at Enid's yard, signs of deprivation and rather desperate attempts to halt the decline evident everywhere. He was pleased at the outcome of his visit but not overly surprised. Left alone with a woman, Pender thought, he could nearly always get his own way, although he had known that Enid Glazzard would test his powers of persuasion more than most.

As Pender Woodvine carried bottles of gin and sherry into Enid's house, he had no idea that he had been led into the very situation that Enid had envisaged. They drank a toast to Girlie's recuperation, each delighted at their own cleverness.

Maisie was showing Girlie Eustace the photograph of Lawry which she had sprung on Dove earlier that morning. Girlie knew what was expected of her but chose instead to say how well Lawry was looking, and how happy.

'That's not the point, Girlie. Just look at the woman with him. She's young enough to be his daughter – not suitable in any way at all.'

'Oh, Maisie,' Girlie's voice was amused, 'why would he want to marry an old woman? And she looks as if she knows how to enjoy herself, which is more than Virginia ever did.' Girlie inspected more closely the picture which Maisie had placed on her lap, touching it gently with her one good hand. 'I think you should wait to meet her before you condemn her; you might even like her.'

Maisie knew that Girlie was right but chose to say, 'You're being very aggravating today.'

Girlie laughed; a little, lopsided laugh. 'I know, darling,

but I always have been. It's just that you are less tolerant than you used to be and you notice it more nowadays: it must be that you're getting old.'

They heard the rattle of knives and forks and glasses and Maisie rose to her feet a little unsteadily to hold open the door for Enid. The trolley which Enid was manoeuvring from the kitchen to the sitting room had previously gouged a channel in the door where a wheel had regularly caught the paintwork. Maisie arrived at the door too late for avoidance and watched while more flakes fluttered onto the carpet, Enid quite unaware that she was the instrument of exasperation.

While Enid put out plates of chicken and salad, Maisie helped Girlie to the nearest chair, seating herself at the further side of the table, so that Enid was nearest to the door and able more easily to go to and from the kitchen to collect those things which she had neglected to bring in the first place and, later, to replace the empty plates with dishes of junket and a cut-glass bowl of clotted cream.

Girlie was aware of Maisie's ill humour, aware also of its cause, trying her best to lift the atmosphere of which Enid, in any case, seemed to be unaware. Enid had yet to be told of Lawry's imminent arrival with his unsuitable bride, as Maisie had relayed this news to Girlie while Enid had been busy in the kitchen. The fact that Maisie treated Enid with just the slightest hint of condescension was an unresolved difficulty for Girlie.

Enid, somewhat to Girlie's surprise, had proved to be an amiable and amusing companion as well as the most resilient of carers, and sometimes Girlie did wonder if, perhaps, Maisie resented their closeness. For years, Maisie and Girlie had lunched together every Thursday before meeting like minded acquaintances for an afternoon of bridge, and later on over gin and tonic the dissection of the foibles of other, absent friends. Maisie and Girlie tried never to be missing at the same time from these afternoons, knowing only too well that one of them needed to be present to prevent both of them from being examined and discussed, either emerging with her reputation just slightly less secure than before. Both were too popular to be subjected to the full force of these observations, but no one escaped the censure of the bridge-playing circle and Enid's arrival as the companion of Girlie Eustace had filled many a drawing room with speculation and innuendo.

For a while after her stroke, Girlie had been forced into the position of onlooker on Thursday afternoons and when it became obvious that she had progressed to that point which was to be her optimum state of mobility, Pender saw that something needed to be done. He devised, and produced with a flourish, a wooden rack curved in a half-circle and fitted with a support and retaining bar into which Girlie could place her cards and which enabled her to take her place at the table as she had always done. Another player dealt for her and never once did Maisie or Enid show any impatience with her now annoyingly protracted deliberations.

Sometimes Pender would join them; occasionally Dove would make up a reluctant fourth but she played distractedly as if her mind were occupied with a list of the weekend shopping or the letters she wrote with such diligence to friends who lived abroad and to whom she remained resolutely attached. Gradually Thursday afternoons became less and less concerned with bridge, lapsing gently and almost imperceptibly into a time of gossip and the covert, disclaimed dozing of elderly women.

It wasn't often that something as entertaining as the second marriage of Maisie's son was provided as the afternoon diversion and when lunch was over and Girlie slept in her upright chair, Maisie and Enid washed and dried the few dishes and settled down with Lawry's indistinct photograph to speculate on his visit. Any small resentment on Maisie's part at the importance that Enid now held in the life of their mutual friend was put aside in her eagerness to recruit another supporter in her censure of her son's choice of wife.

3

Dove saw Enid's car leaving early enough to enable her to drive home in daylight. Now that the days were shortening Girlie preferred not to be out in the dimpsey, that period which was neither light nor dark, as she thought, mistakenly, that it worried Enid. Enid drove like a man; taught by her oldest brother and proud of her clean record, she was audacious and confident but allowed Girlie the pretext of anxiety on her behalf.

Dove waited a little while and then went to collect her mother's tablets from the dining room where she had left them that morning, and as she picked up the bag of crochet cotton she saw again the spite in Cissy Beckerleg's eyes as she had enquired with spurious sympathy about Dove's welfare. Dove understood the subtlety of the blackmail which encouraged Maisie to continue to buy her wool and crochet cotton at the little, old-fashioned shop, although the new shop in Truro had such good quality yarns and the colours were so subtle and appealing that Dove would gladly have driven much further just to avoid the Beckerleg sisters. Maisie, though, stuck unwaveringly to their stock of bright acrylics which she knitted into squares before stitching them together to make blankets which were sent overseas by Oxfam. The crochet cotton was translated into mats of intricacy and charm which were Maisie's contribution to the handicrafts stall at St John Bosco's annual Summer Fayre and which always sold out at once. Maisie had always resisted making money out of her hobby and her work was still as fine and even as it had always been, her fingers seeming to move without thought or guidance as she watched television, the intricate lacework depending from her hands.

The room where Maisie sat was almost dark when Dove walked in, only one side lamp lit and even this bulb flickered and went out as Dove approached. She was surprised that the television wasn't on and more surprised still to see her mother sitting, hands idle in her lap. 'Tablets, cotton.' Dove placed them on the low table next to Maisie's chair and then went to find a replacement light bulb. When she came back Maisie was still just as she had left her and Dove said, 'Good afternoon? Did you play any bridge?'

Maisie pushed herself more upright in her chair and looked at her daughter without speaking. Then she stretched out a thin hand and laid it on Dove's. 'What would I do without you? Thank you, darling.'

There was another silence, Dove not sure how to respond, the self-deprecating answer that had risen to her lips suddenly inappropriate as she looked at her mother's face. 'Is something wrong, Maisie? Girlie's not ill or anything, is she? Enid all right?'

'Oh, they're perfectly well; Girlie was in good form actually, although she was being rather aggravating.'

'But?'

'But,' Maisie gave a small smile, lowering her head so that Dove only half imagined that she saw it, 'but I'm a silly old woman and I was sitting here thinking about how good you are to me and how that thoughtless brother of yours can pull a trick that has us all running around like headless chickens.'

'Hardly, Maisie, I've already got their room ready and it's only two more to feed.'

'That's *just* what I mean. He turns up without any thought for what we may be doing or whether it's convenient and we just get on with it, accommodating him and the child bride as if it's a privilege he's bestowed on us. He might, at least, have asked.'

'When did he ever?' Dove was walking around the room. She drew the curtains and picked up the empty glasses, balancing in her other hand the small discarded dishes which had held prawn crackers and crisps. They still gave off a trace of synthetic seasoning and Dove turned her head aside, wondering again how three old women could enjoy such ersatz flavours.

She had almost given up trying to persuade Maisie to exchange her butter and full cream milk for healthier alternatives and had to accept, unwillingly, that her mother actually preferred bacon fried in fat to that grilled and drained as Dove now prepared it. Maisie still drank what to Dove appeared to be far too much gin, and at every opportunity she ate impressive amounts of puddings full of cream and cholesterol.

Maisie had stopped smoking at seventy-five, mainly because she was inclined to fall into a light doze with a cigarette still burning between her fingers. The last time this had happened Dove had been awfully angry and had insisted on having smoke alarms installed, which she checked regularly to make sure that they were still functioning. Maisie hated the obtrusive blank look of these unwanted sentinels and allowed an unnecessarily long shriek to continue on the odd occasion when Pender's smoke activated one of them. Dove had pointed out to Maisie the childishness of this game, emphasising patiently that in the event of a real fire, she might choose to ignore the warning.

Maisie had placated her daughter, telling her that she would speak to Pender about it but wondering from where Dove had inherited a streak of such assiduous responsibility. Perhaps, she thought, if Eddie had lived instead of being blown up in that minesweeper when he was still only thirty, he might have developed this sobriety, this absolute predictability, which she found so tedious in her daughter.

Now Maisie looked at Dove and saw a tired, middle-aged woman who was watching her with concern. Maisie knew that the feeling was genuine but she longed to tell her daughter that she had no need to allow anxiety to encroach upon their relationship; that even at eighty life was exciting and each day brought some small entertainment to be savoured and stored away for sharing with Pender or Girlie.

She didn't say any of this but said, instead, 'I feel it's my fault, you see. I must have spoiled him; let him get away with things that I'd not have allowed in you.'

Dove spoke slowly, not wanting the long buried resentment she felt at being her mother's less favoured child to slip, uncontrolled, into the dusky corners of the inadequately lit room. 'It's different with a boy, I suppose. I think,' she hesitated, 'I think you *did* treat us differently, but so did Granny and Papa Woodvine when we lived with them. I think it was so awful for them when Uncle Grenfell died that they wanted to believe that Lawry could take his place and then, when Eddie died as well, he was the only male left in the next generation so, of course, they spoiled him.'

Dove had never known how to refer to her father: 'Daddy' seemed too childish in a woman of fifty-four; 'Dad', as if they had been together long enough to become companions, familiar, easy with each other; and 'Father' too confusing in a household where the Reverend Dick O'Brian regularly dropped in to see Pender for a reviving shot of Irish and some advice on the week's runners. She had decided that to refer to Eddie Eustace by his christian name was the most suitable way round the problem – but even this she found difficult.

She thought of her three daughters and how each one had been inspected and then gently dismissed by her own grandmother, Verena Woodvine, who had left Dove under no misapprehension that she had failed each time by not producing a son to replace the young men lost in the war. Verena had never allowed her great-granddaughters to know that they were a disappointment to her, but always perceptible to Dove was the anticipation of Lawry's sons. Lawry's sons who were never born, nor daughters, for he and Virginia had no children and Verena had died a few months after Jossy's birth, unreconciled to the fact that there were no boys left in the family. Now, Dove thought, with Lawry's late marriage, perhaps he will have a son after all. She found the idea distasteful: her brother, two years older than her, burdened by disorder and broken nights with a young child.

'Something's amusing you.' Maisie had been watching Dove as she tidied the room. When she could find no more to do she had sat down in the chair opposite her mother's, not speaking, weary but with a feeling of accomplishment after a day when she seemed to have worked without respite at one tiresome task after another.

'I was thinking about Lawry.'

'And that amused you? I wish *I* felt like that.'

'What I found diverting was the thought that he might become a father even now. Imagine Lawry surrounded by nappies and bottles and sick.' Dove's smile widened into real amusement and she looked at her mother. 'Perhaps he'll have the boy that Granny Woodvine always wanted so.'

'Oh, Dove darling, you shouldn't have known that. She did love the little girls and she tried not to show how much she wanted a grandson. It was losing Grenfell you see; he was her beloved son and she never became accustomed to his absence.' Maisie stretched her hands along the worn arms of the chair, curling her fingers over the edge where the fullness of the material was caught in pleats by small brass nails hammered into the cloth. 'She was fond of Pender, of course, but he was never quite the same to her, and if you feel sorry for anyone it should be for him. No matter what he did, he couldn't take Grenfell's place and he knew it, but Verena thought a grandson would be different.' Maisie leaned back in her chair, where one of her crocheted squares protected the velvet from wear. In the dim light her hair gave the illusion of being dark again, the soft wrinkles on her face erased and Dove was confused for a moment into thinking that her mother was still young. 'I always thought it was a good thing that you had girls as she might have given a boy the legacy of inadequacy that poor old Pen's always had to contend with.'

Dove thought about this in the quiet room where the only sound was a gentle soughing from the radiator and before she allowed herself to submit to the drowsiness which seemed to overcome her these days if she sat down in the afternoon, she made a mental note to ask Lewis to look at the heating system as she supposed there must be an air lock causing the noise. Maisie looked at her daughter and remained still, knowing her evening programme was about to start but not moving to turn on the television.

Dove woke with a start as Sandy sidled into the room, too late for Maisie to divert him. The dog made straight for Dove who was sitting in Pender's usual chair and began to lick her hand, his rough tongue wet and persistent. Dove pulled her hand away at once and pushed Sandy towards Pender, who had followed him into the room. 'What's up? Dark as a tomb in here.' He turned on the main light and caught Sandy by the collar, pulling him down to the carpet.

'Stay there, old boy, you know that Aunty Dove doesn't like you.'

Dove stood up, smoothed the cushion against which she had been resting and looked at her uncle. 'Hello, Pen. Had a good walk?'

'Whatever gave you the idea that I've been walking?' His hand disappeared in the long hair on Sandy's back as he looked at Dove. 'Better things to do than walk, even at my age.' He smiled the smile he thought of as rakish: his often remarked-on resemblance to Maurice Chevalier allowing him the illusion that he was a playboy, a boulevardier, a roué. 'Oh yes, much better things.'

Dove, not yet quite in command of herself after having been woken so precipitately, looked at her uncle with disapproval. 'If by "better things" you mean that dreadful little Mrs Fielding, I don't want to hear about it. And Sandy needs a bath, he's smelling terrible.' She turned towards her mother. 'See you later, Maisie. About ten?' Dove paused in the doorway. 'I nearly forgot to ask you – Lawry's wife, what's her name, Maisie?'

Maisie looked down for a minute and then at Dove, hesitating a little before she answered, 'She's called Loretta.'

'I see. And does she sing country and western songs as well as everything else?'

'I don't understand.'

'Oh, never mind.'

Maisie heard the back door close. 'She's been running around all day getting things ready for Lawry and the child bride and she's tired, Pen. I'm sure she didn't mean to be unkind.'

'No. No, I don't suppose she did.' He took the chair that Dove had been sitting in. 'Am I an old fool, Maisie?'

'Of course you are, but those of us who know and love you wouldn't have you any other way and why should the young have all the fun?'

'Perhaps that's what's wrong with Dove; needs a bit of fun, lighten her up a bit. Don't get me wrong, old girl, I'm forever grateful to her because who else would put up with us and look after us the way she does, but I wouldn't mind a bit of healthy neglect if I thought that she enjoyed her life a bit more.'

'I sometimes think that Dove was born middle-aged. Do you suppose she gets it from her father? You knew Eddie for much longer than I did – do you recall him as sober and conscientious? We had such a short time together that I remember most of it as such fun, especially the summer before the war started.' Maisie's fingers smoothed the material on the arms of the chair, over and over, her nails painted the same old rose colour as the velvet.

She could see Eddie Eustace, tall and always amiable, with the same dark gold hair as Dove which neither ever managed quite to subdue. That summer Lawry had been old enough to enjoy the beach and Eddie had dug castles in the sand and had carried the little boy on his shoulders, a knight surveying his demesne from the safety of his charger. Eddie had pointed out to his son the bowers and battlements, the outer bailey and the enclosure wall, and together they had tried to stop the moat from filling with water which slowly undermined the sandy foundations until the castle crumbled and slid gently under the incoming waves.

Lawry had not understood where his plaything had gone and Eddie had lifted him high into the air above his head. 'Don't you worry, old chap, there's always tomorrow: we'll build a bigger, better one tomorrow and we'll buy a packet of flags to stick on every turret. How about that?'

Maisie had felt no more than a faint disturbance at the knowledge that the days of castles on the beach were ending and that before the child she was carrying would be born, Eddie would have joined the navy and she would be managing on her own. Eddie could have stayed at home, his occupation reserved as vital to the war effort, but neither he nor Maisie considered this justification for not volunteering. Maisie, who had taken a secretarial course before she was married, was prepared to take over running the business in Eddie's absence working under the direction of the Ministry of Food. Pender was declared unfit for military service, and when he joined her at Eustace and Sons Maisie had found life as a business woman far more fulfilling than that of the mother of two small children. The local girl she had engaged as a nanny left to go into a munitions factory and Maisie hadn't bothered to look for a replacement but had sent Lawry and Dove to her parents, Verena and Matabele Jack Woodvine. The children were well looked after at Rejerrah and there they had lived until the end of the war.

Dove had started peeling potatoes for the evening meal before she saw the note in Lewis's writing propped against a sponge ware jug on the dresser. The words scribbled in the same mauve pen that she had used earlier in the day told her that Diana had 'phoned and would try again later when her mother was in. Dove went to find a cauliflower, vaguely apprehensive. Diana, the oldest of her daughters, was a constant source of worry to Dove. Clever, bossy and intractable, she had married straight from university: 'sweeping that poor young man along in her slipstream,' Maisie had said, but Luke had remained besotted with Diana, admiring her drive and seeming not to mind always having to be the one who gave way in an argument. Until, that is, they started to discuss starting a family: Luke wanted children, Diana did not.

'It's so unfair,' she had told Dove, 'I *never* said that I wanted children. I didn't even pretend that I might change my mind and he *knew* that, right from the beginning. Nothing's changed so he might as well accept that right now.'

'But, darling,' Dove had tried to find the right words, 'you say that now but you may feel differently in a few years' time and you're still young. Couldn't you just try not to be quite so adamant. Luke does have a right to his opinion, you know, and most men do want a proper family.'

'For goodness' sake, Mother, haven't you been listening at all? There's no chance of me having children and Luke should have married someone else if he wanted what you call "a proper family".'

'In that case, you'll probably lose him. Have you thought of that?'

'Of course, but if he wants to choose some imaginary idyll over me, then that's the way it will be. I'll manage, just as Granny Maisie did when Eddie died, and Great-Granny Verena lived for twenty-five years on her own, didn't she?'

There had been more outbursts, more recriminations, but Diana had never cried and Dove wondered at her lack of perceptible sorrow at the situation. Now, with this 'phone call, Dove feared that some decision had been reached, some conclusive action taken which would impose on the family adjustments which she knew that she would find difficult to encompass at any time, and almost too demanding just at the moment.

As Dove cut away the outer leaves of the cauliflower she tried to concentrate on what she was doing, to anchor her mind on the mundane. If she let her thoughts slip like a kite string from her grasp she knew that pursuit would be useless. Worries about Diana; unanswered questions about Lawry and his unsuitable wife, trickled and insinuated their way like some viscous stream around the problems already in her mind: Pender and his latest attachment to the young and fatuous Anita Fielding; the definition of Dove's own days by her mother's need for her, seemed at times more than she could bear.

Dove allowed small fragments of thought to swim into her mind, but as she traced the convoluted pattern on the head of the cauliflower she suppressed the knowledge that underlay most of her unease. She had often thought that a cauliflower looked like a brain and now she cut deeply into the sweet, white stalk as if by cutting through the spinal cord she could detach her thoughts from the knowledge that her husband no longer loved her.

As she separated the florets, dropping them into her old, battered, colander the 'phone rang again. Dove waited to see if Lewis was in and would pick up the extension in his study but the shrilling went on and she wiped her hands down the front of her pinafore and went to answer it. It was Diana, as she had thought it would be: her daughter was coming home, would arrive just after lunch the next day and would be staying until she had decided what to do next.

Dove sat down at the kitchen table, her hand across her mouth as if to hold back the words she wanted to say: that Diana had a perfectly good home in which she should stay with her own husband and that she, Dove, was too tired to have to assimilate another person into the already overfull household and that she wanted time for herself, to try to understand what was happening in the suddenly precarious fragility of her life.

4

Diana arrived the next afternoon just as Dove had settled down with a mug of tea and the newspapers. She had taken them into her favourite room which was off the kitchen and it was here that she had a roll-top desk and a shelf of cookery books and where she kept on display home-made presents from the children, treasured since they were small: a stone painted with a cat's face, the tin covered with wallpaper for spare pens, a mobile made from old beads and buttons. There were comfortable chairs in this room and a sofa, large and deep and soft, and, with a cushion behind her head, Dove often napped here for a while when her work was done. Years ago, when it had been new, the sofa had been covered in linen of dark emerald and navy blue to match the curtains but the impression it gave now was of a silvery, threadbare grey.

Dove had never been very much concerned with decorating the house and now, looking around in anticipation of her new sister-in-law's reaction, she realised with amazement how shabby and eccentric an impression pervaded the familiar rooms. The curtains here had a wide bleached stripe along the edge nearest the window and Dove noticed for the first time that the small Sutherland table which had belonged to Verena was faded in a line matching exactly the position of the windowsill: the fierce sun in this part of the country stole colour from everything, leaving fabric and furniture blanched and pale, but it was something that Dove was so used to that she gave it no thought.

Her hand traced the tulipwood star inlaid in the narrow top of the table and she thought idly that she should do something about it, concentrating instead on the earliest anemones which she had picked yesterday and brought into the warmth of the house, their flat pinkish-green stems visible through the sides of the clear vase into which she had put them. Dove loved anemones almost better than anything else, flowering bravely in the cold; sooty black stamens powdering into a circle around the purple and red petals. She always tried to have flowers of some sort in this room and Pender, knowing her passion, kept her supplied in the summer with sweet peas and cornflowers, marigolds, love-in-a-mist or lady's mantle; unsophisticated, old-fashioned plants with which he had filled the garden he shared with Maisie.

Dove settled into the soft folds of the sofa, pushing aside magazines and books to enable her to rest her feet on the top of a long stool. She was flicking through the paper to see if anything seemed worth the effort of concentration when a car drew up outside. From the noise of the abrupt way in which it stopped and the way in which the door was slammed she knew it to be Diana and knew also that she was going to have to call on reserves of energy which she had come to understand were not infinite as she had for so long believed.

Dove heard her daughter's progress through the house: the front door closing, a rattle as Diana threw her car keys and handbag onto the hall table, footsteps into the kitchen and the sound of water rushing out of the tap. Dove had forgotten how much water Diana drank and she pictured her now, standing at the sink, letting the water run until it was cold enough and then drinking two full glasses before wiping her mouth on the heel of her hand, not even noticing where the Niagara of water had splashed and settled in pools on the shiny surfaces Dove had so recently cleaned.

'In here, darling.' Dove put aside the *Mail* but didn't move from her comfortable position, lifting up her face for Diana's kiss. 'Good journey?'

'Not very.' Diana, small and dark, so like Lewis that Dove was always surprised each time she saw her after an absence, stood looking at her mother. 'I've left Luke and I've come home to sort out what I'm going to do. Is there anything to eat? I'm starving.'

Dove felt a surge of anger that seemed as if it were about to become visible, to leap from her in tangible form, speaking words which she would surely regret but which no one would accept were not of her volition. She struggled to make her voice appear normal. 'Cheese, ham, salad – make yourself a sandwich. The tea's probably still hot, it's not long since I made it.' She wondered if she should say something about Luke, but Diana had turned abruptly and gone into the kitchen. Dove heard her clattering about and wondered why, of all three girls, only the chaos generated by Diana affected her the way it did. Dove wished that Lewis was at home; he understood Diana much better than Dove had ever done and he, if anyone, would be able to make some sense of what was going on.

Diana came back and sat at Dove's desk, moving a cookery book and some recipe notes that Dove had been working on to clear a space for her pile of sandwiches and a mug of tea. When she had eaten several of the sandwiches she turned to Dove. 'Aren't you going to say anything?'

'What do you want me to say? I don't know enough about the situation to make any useful comment.'

'That doesn't usually stop you.'

'That's not fair, Diana, nor is it true.' The angry being in

Dove threatened again to become manifest, but her voice was mild.

'Sorry, I think I've just got used to hurting people and I can't stop. I've been really horrible to Luke and he doesn't deserve it.' Dove looked up but Diana went on, 'No, don't even hope that I'll change my mind and go back, because I won't. I know it's not ideal to land myself on you but I didn't know what else to do.' After a pause she said, 'Chucked in my job as well.'

'Oh, Diana, I don't know what to say.'

'Let's just leave it and I'll talk to Dad sometime, it's no big deal anyway.' Diana finished the pile of sandwiches before saying, 'I think I'll go and have a shower and unpack.'

She walked towards the door but Dove, suddenly alert, said, 'Just a minute, Di, I haven't had time to make up your bed or do anything to the room. I've been too busy getting ready for Uncle Lawry and,' Dove took a breath, 'and Loretta.'

'And who is Loretta?'

'Uncle Lawry's wife.'

'Oh great; you might have warned me that the house would be full of guests.' Diana added as an afterthought, 'And you didn't tell me that he'd got married, so how was I supposed to know who Loretta is?'

'We've only just found out ourselves, he has rather sprung it on us.' Dove could no longer suppress her annoyance and as she collected Diana's plate and mug from her desk, she added, 'A bit like you leaving Luke really.'

Diana fetched a backpack and two large canvas holdalls from her car, leaving them at the bottom of the stairs before going back for black plastic sacks and several boxes overflowing with books and compact discs. Dove, bemused, didn't offer to help and felt an undercurrent of disquiet which she knew was a recognition of her own weakness in the face of Diana's uncompromising self-assurance; the knowledge that her presence would be welcome in her parents' home a certainty she had never thought to question.

Dove blamed Lewis for the difficulty she had always had in reconciling herself to what she saw as Diana's unaccommodating directness. He had seen in their eldest daughter the strength and determination not to be side-tracked that had always eluded him and he had encouraged her ambition to become a civil engineer. Dove was aware of her exclusion from their mutual attachment and felt shame at her sense of relief when Diana had left home to go to university. She loved her difficult daughter as deeply as the two younger girls but had singularly failed to recognise in Diana a reflection of her own certitude that her way was right and therefore appropriate and non-negotiable. There was also, of course, their mutual, unacknowledged contrition.

It was unfortunate that Lewis chose the evening of Diana's return to be late home from work. Almost invariably he arrived at six-thirty, Dove cooked for seven o'clock and had the dishes washed and the kitchen tidy by eight. She had made a cottage pie and had left it in the oven with the heat turned down while she drained and chopped cabbage and spread butter and parsley on the carrots. Lewis was fond of puddings and there was clafoutis to follow, made with cherries that Dove had bottled in early July.

Diana had come into the kitchen, watching her mother in silence. Dove moved her gently away from the drawer where she kept her sharp knives. 'I don't know where your father is, it's not like him to be late and I did hope he'd be early today. He'll be so pleased to see you, he does miss you.' She added quickly, 'Bethan, too, of course but we see more of her.'

'Is she still with that awful man – Geoffrey? Joseph?'

'Julius.'

'Worse.'

'Now, don't start Diana! We like Julius very much. He's kind and considerate and takes such good care of Bethan.'

'I'm not surprised you like him; after all, he's nearer your age than Bethan's. I suppose you'd say that Luke is kind and considerate too?'

'I've no reason to believe otherwise, and the fact that you've left him doesn't alter our opinion of him.' Dove scraped the cabbage into a vegetable dish which she put into the oven to keep warm with the pie. 'It's difficult for us too, you know. Luke is our son-in-law and we're both very fond of him; you can't expect us to cut him off completely because you no longer want to be married to him. I suppose we shall lose touch; he'll marry again and disappear from our lives, but I shan't *forget* him, if that's what you're hoping. I like Luke you see, that's the difference.' Dove moved Diana again, this time away from the sink, where she was now leaning, picking hot carrot rings out of the strainer and eating them, one by one. Dove's touch told her how thin her daughter was, the bones in her hip seeming almost naked under Dove's hand. It saddened her and she spoke to her less sharply: 'You could chop the parsley for me.' Dove passed Diana the long knife she used and, quickly and competently, Diana dealt with the aromatic leaves, watching the juice seep out under the pressure of the blade, staining the wooden chopping board. She ate a sprig and scattered the rest on the butter, now melting over the carrots.

'Do we have to wait for Daddy and Joss?'

'Of course. If you feel like it you could make a start on the pans while we're waiting and then there won't be so much to do later on. And you ought just to go and say hello to your grandmother.'

It was as if Diana hadn't heard a word: Dove wondered

for a minute if she had actually spoken aloud at all as she watched her daughter walk out of the kitchen and heard the television coming on in the room next door. Vexed and resigned, Dove pulled on her rubber gloves and started to run water into the washing-up bowl.

At seven-thirty Lewis found that he had to manoeuvre around Diana's little Renault to park his own car. He was pleased at the thought of seeing her and grateful for the diversion her presence would cause. As he passed Maisie's back door, Jossy came out, calling goodbye to her grandmother. She walked beside her father without asking why he was so late. 'Diana's home.'

'I know. Saw the car – parked skewwhiff as usual. I'll move them around later on.'

'She's quite capable of doing it herself, but I don't suppose she'll bother.'

Lewis stopped walking and looked at his youngest daughter. 'That doesn't sound like you, Jossy. Something the matter?' They had arrived at the back door and Lewis put out his hand to feel for the handle. He could cope with Diana's dauntless belief in her own capabilities – he had, after all, lived with Dove for nearly thirty years – and with Bethan's independence and unconventional opinions, but Jossy, so like him, but quieter and so private, confused him. He sometimes suspected that she wasn't very happy but it wasn't something he discussed with Dove, feeling inadequate to withstand what he felt sure would be her confident assurances that all was well with their daughter.

Jossy smiled at her father. 'What d'you think? Mum's in a tizz about meeting Uncle Lawry's new wife anyway, and now that Diana's moved back in the atmosphere's a bit on the fraught side. I was afraid it might be contagious so I escaped to Granny's until I heard your car arrive. It wasn't much better there actually; seems Uncle Pen's got a new ladyfriend, but I expect you knew that, didn't you?' She looked sideways at Lewis, his face carefully impassive as he opened the door and stood aside for her to go in.

'What do you mean by, "Diana's moved back in"? Isn't she just here on a visit?'

Jossy shook her head. 'She's finally left Luke and she's brought her half of the marital home with her from the look of it.'

'Oh!'

Dove appeared in the kitchen doorway. 'We were just going to start without you: I expect everything's spoiled anyway.'

'What you need is a microwave.'

'What I need is for everyone to be on time, or at least to let me know if they're going to be late.' Dove put the cottage pie and vegetables on the table: they were all, deliberately, slightly too crisp and Lewis exchanged a look with Diana as Dove went back to the hob to warm up the gravy. 'Where were you, Lewis?'

'Doing a little job for Pender,' Lewis said, but not before Jossy had seen the same look eclipse his natural expression that she had first noticed outside the back door. 'Don't be cross, cariad; not on Diana's first night home.' He put his hand over Diana's thin brown fingers and squeezed them gently. 'How long are you staying, lovely girl?'

Dove turned around with the jug of gravy in her hand. In thirty years of marriage she had learned two things and one of them was that when Lewis started to sound like Richard Burton he was either drunk or concealing something. She put the gravy down and looked at her husband. He certainly wasn't drunk.

They were eating in the kitchen and a faint smell of cabbage and overcooked potato hung in the air. It was not altogether agreeable, like an unheard echo of the thoughts of the family around the table. Lewis, alone, seemed untroubled by the edgy silences broken by the most prosaic of conversation. Had Diana come by motorway and how long had it taken her? Was Jossy going shopping with Maisie tomorrow to look for shoes? It was as if they had entered into an unspoken agreement not to mention Luke, or Pender's friend; to ignore Lewis's absence earlier in the evening. There would be time for all that later on and Dove watched Diana pushing her food around, moving a forkful of cabbage behind a pile of carrots, separating meat from potato and eating neither. As soon as everyone had finished, Diana gathered all the plates together in an attempt to hide from her mother just how little she herself had eaten.

Dove knew better than to press Diana into eating, having learned over the years that she would graze steadily all evening; crisps, half an apple, a bowl of cornflakes, perhaps making herself cheese on toast which she would taste and then throw into the compost bin. It was a pattern which Diana had followed since her early teens and was the catalyst for many of the most grievous misunderstandings between them. Now Dove, alarmed and disturbed by the fragility of Diana's body, pretended not to notice the deception and passed her as large a slice of pudding as she gave to Jossy, moving the cream towards her with a smile.

Lewis pronounced the clafoutis a triumph and when Dove got up to make coffee, he quietly swopped his empty plate for Diana's, eating the second helping with as much enjoyment as the first. Diana pushed her chair back. 'I'd better go and see Granny; get the gossip on Uncle Lawry and this Loretta.' Her face was mischievous. 'Do you suppose that she's got a long blonde wig and a background of rural perversion?'

'For pity's sake don't talk like that in front of your grandmother, she's touchy enough about it as it is.' Dove couldn't altogether suppress a smile, the silent simper of the woman in the photograph that Maisie had concealed, had disturbed her with its suggestion of unrestrained gratification.

'A joke, Mum.'

'Of course. Try and get an early night, darling, you look all in.'

Diana went out and Jossy started to sort plates and cutlery into a rational order for washing up. 'You sit down, Mummy, you've had a hard day and you know I don't mind doing it.' It was true: even as a small child Jossy had enjoyed standing on a chair with one of Dove's pinafores tied around her, swirling and swishing the water, watching rainbow-coloured bubbles froth and disperse as she conscientiously cleaned every tine of every fork, running her hands over the plates to make sure no lingering particle of dried-on food was left. When she had finished she would wipe the taps and dry the sink, making sure that the plughole was clear of detritus, before going up to Dove and kissing her. Dove had expected this odd gesture to stop as Jossy grew up but it was as if it were a necessary part of the ritual, without which the exercise was incomplete.

Dove put the coffee cups on the draining board. 'I thought I'd see if Bethan and Julius would like to come for the day on Sunday, to see Uncle Lawry and to meet Loretta.'

'Hadn't you better wait and see what Uncle Lawry wants to do? They may have plans of their own.' Jossy rinsed out the cups before putting them into the bowl. 'Granny showed me the photo; I thought Loretta looked quite nice.'

'Oh, Jossy, you always think that everyone's nice.'

'No, I don't.' Jossy rested her hands on the edge of the sink and looked out of the window. All she could see was a reflection of herself and Dove, isolated and indistinct in the darkness outside in the winter garden. 'I don't think that Anita Fielding's nice. I think she's detestable, a hypocrite, and I wish Uncle Pen'd never met her.'

Dove looked at her in silence, taken aback by the vehemence in Jossy's gentle voice. 'Do you know her? I hardly do, although from the little I've seen of her I suppose I'd describe her as a silly woman. But a hypocrite?'

'She's not just silly, Mum, she's dangerous.'

'That's the trouble with silly people, they often are; but Pender's little dalliances are never too serious and I'm sure she'll soon get tired of him and find someone more exciting.'

Jossy looked at her mother's diminished reflection in the glass for a long time and then turned her head towards Dove, plunging yellow rubber hands into the water once more. 'I'm sure you're right, but I still don't like her. And I don't trust her either, not for a minute.'

Lawry and Loretta arrived two days later – one day earlier than they were expected. Dove was in the garden with Maisie, clearing away the dismal reminders of late autumn flowers, when they heard a car drive around the side of the house and stop by the back door. Dove continued to hack at the hard brown stalks of perennial sunflowers and to throw them onto a pile she was generating on the path, imagining, if she thought about it at all, that it was the girls returning from Porthlevan, Diana having announced at breakfast that they were going out and not to expect either of them for lunch.

Maisie had eaten with Dove, a cooked chicken from Marks & Spencers and a chocolate Swiss roll. Maisie was unusually quiet and Dove, understanding her mother's apprehension, put aside her own misgivings to ensure that, for a while at least, no concern should intrude on their pleasure. They had lunch together once or twice a week and Dove made an effort to give her mother food that she knew she would particularly enjoy. Her mother understood that it was Dove's way of showing feelings which she would have found difficult to express in words and although sometimes Maisie would have preferred just a bowl of bread and milk or some tinned soup, she was resolutely grateful to Dove and ate rather more than she needed with every appearance of enjoyment.

Maisie was wearing the new shoes that Jossy had taken her into Truro to buy, and as she wiped her mouth after clearing the last crumbs of cake from her plate, she said, 'I suppose it's like knickers really.'

Dove, who was becoming used to the vagaries of her mother's conversation as Maisie increasingly finished sentences aloud which she had previously conducted silently with herself, tried to make some sort of connection between knickers and the delicatessen in Truro from which Jossy had chosen several pieces of cheese to bring home, the merits of which Dove and Maisie had been discussing some minutes before.

'Cheese?'

'Shoes, darling: shoes are like knickers, something you buy to cheer yourself up.'

'Are they? I only buy shoes when I need a pair.' Dove thought for a moment. 'And I don't buy knickers to cheer me up, either.'

Maisie looked at Dove and smiled, the wrinkles around her eyes deepening and coalescing so that her cheeks looked like the map of a river delta. 'What *do* you buy then, when you want to spoil yourself? I've often wondered.'

Dove pulled the Swiss roll towards her and cut another slice as if unaware of what she was doing. She unravelled an inch or two as she had done when she was a child and then looked at Maisie, clandestine prawn sandwiches banished beyond her mother's enquiring gaze. 'Perhaps I don't need to buy anything; have you thought of that?'

'Of course you do; everyone does. Take Pender, for instance, he buys seeds. Or, if he's really down, a plant. Or two. With Girlie, it's scent: the more expensive the bottle, the bluer she is. Often, she doesn't actually *use* it

– in fact she gives most of it away as raffle prizes – but it's something she needs to do now and again.'

'How extraordinary.' Dove was sure that her mother was right and was struck once more at how much the older woman observed.

'Not at all.' Maisie looked sideways at Dove. 'What about all those notebooks and pens you have? Enough to stock a medium sized branch of W H Smith I should think.' She didn't mention the sandwiches, or the fluted plastic pots of fanciful yoghurt, that she was well aware of Dove concealing in the dustbin.

Dove finished her cake, wishing that she hadn't started to eat it in the first place but quite unable to leave something untouched on her plate. It reminded her of Diana and the old, familiar prick of concern seized her. 'You're right, Maisie, I hadn't thought of it like that and now that I have, I shan't be able to buy another ever again without feeling guilty.'

'That's the difference between us, Dove darling, I *never* feel guilty about anything and you seem to carry such a burden around with you.' Maisie hesitated, unwilling to intrude into areas around which there were unacknowledged boundaries. 'If there was something really wrong, you would tell me, wouldn't you?' Dove was silent and Maisie went on, 'Is it me and Pen, are we too much for you? We've always known we might have to make other arrangements one day. You just have to say.'

'Of course it's not. Oh, Maisie, of course it's not and please don't talk like that because it's nonsense and you know it.' Dove made an effort to explain. 'There's nothing really; it's just that so much seems to be happening at once and I never have quite enough time to catch up. I get a bit tired, that's all.'

'You need some help in the house.'

'You sound like Lewis.'

'What did he suggest?'

'Oh, you know, usual things. Getting someone in to help with the housework and ironing and perhaps a gardener for a few hours a week.'

'And you said no, I suppose?'

'Well the garden doesn't take much time, except for the grass, and Pender looks after that anyway.' Dove said nothing about the housework but started to collect empty plates, gathering together the four corners of the red gingham tablecloth which she would take outside and shake in the garden. Neither woman would ever mention it, but they both thought of Dove's first helper, Gracie Beckerleg's daughter, Sylvie. From the time that she had left school at fourteen Gracie had worked at Rejerrah for both Verena and Maisie and when Dove's children were small it had seemed natural for Dove to employ Sylvie.

Sylvie was used to the routine of the Courtneys: she had already been helping Gracie for several years with the preparations for the bottling and freezing of vegetables that marked the autumn at Rejerrah, Dove insistent that nothing should be wasted that could be preserved. Sometimes Sylvie joined Dove and the little girls on blackberry picnics and worked all day, filling baskets lined with cabbage leaves with the purple-black berries which, later on, she would turn into jam. One pantry, the old dairy, was full of rows of jewel coloured jars; topaz marmalade, ruby currant, amethyst and garnet fruit jellies; even the lemon curd looked to Sylvie like pale, edible amber.

Dove was fair in her demands of Sylvie, objective in her praise, but there was never any warmth in her acknowledgment of the girl, no question that Sylvie would ever be translated into anything other than someone to whom Dove handed an envelope each Friday afternoon, smiling her thanks for a satisfactory week's work.

If Sylvie was aware of the distance Dove chose to keep

between them, she made no mention of it except to report each evening to Gracie and her Aunt Cissie on every detail of her day at Rejerrah, the two women never seeming to tire of the repeated tedium.

In spite of the satisfactory way in which she fitted into the household, there was something about Sylvie Beckerleg that unsettled Dove. Sometimes, turning in half-light, she would get the unnerving feeling that she had seen herself in the shadows, or Sylvie's teasing laugh when she was playing with the girls seemed to be an echo of one remembered from long ago. Dove thought herself fanciful and for a long time managed to suppress any flights of imagination which threatened to undermine the stability of their relationship. There was, therefore, nothing inevitable about Sylvie's dismissal, although the shock to Dove of her discovery was no less profound than it would have been had she been told the truth when she was young and less reproachful.

In those days Dove had a favourite evening dress, a 1930s black satin cut on the bias, which had once belonged to Maisie. Before Dove began to put on weight it had suited her very well and she wore it occasionally with a bolero of black georgette sprinkled with clusters of silver paillettes, or with Verena's long string of pearls.

One day in the spring when Jossy had been two, Dove had taken her out for a walk, as she did every afternoon between lunch and going to collect her other daughters from school. It was a day of high blue skies, daffodils bending in the wind off the sea and dead palm fronds clashing and rustling on the ground. There had been early rain and Jossy, laughing and running on the toes of her shoes as all small children do, had missed her footing, fallen, and sat looking at Dove, not sure whether to laugh or cry. She decided on neither, pushing her hands further into the mud in an effort to stand up again.

Dove had taken Jossy home, pulling off her small yellow

wellingtons in the back hall and carrying her upstairs to the bathroom which opened off the bedroom she and Lewis shared. The house was quiet in the after lunch lull: Dove could hear *Woman's Hour* on the radio in the kitchen where Sylvie Beckerleg would be ironing, Diana and Bethan still at school.

Dove always kept her bedroom door closed, a barrier of privacy which the children learned early not to breach, and as she turned towards the room with Jossy in her arms, Dove was surprised to see the door standing half-open. She was sure that it was not as she had left it only a short time ago, and she had pushed it wider with her foot.

The long cheval glass reflected back to her the figure of Sylvie Beckerleg wearing the black satin dress and Verena's pearls, the girl's own jeans and hand-knitted jersey thrown casually on the bed as if it were an everyday affair. Dove scarcely hesitated and carried Jossy into the bathroom, peeling off the child's stained cardigan and dungarees, closing the door firmly behind them. Dove washed her gently under the shower, watching the muddy water flow and divide around the little, soft body, resting like raindrops in Jossy's curly hair. Dove took a long time to dry her, patting plump, pink feet with a thick towel, reassuring and maternal. Dove had stared at the cloth with so much concentration that, even now, she could remember that it had been a soft aquamarine colour and that there had been scallop shells around the border. Anything at all not to confront the enormity of what she had just seen.

When Dove shepherded Jossy into the bedroom there was no sign that anyone else had ever been there. She put the child on the bed and very hesitantly opened the right-hand door of the wardrobe. The satin dress was hanging in its cover made from an old sheet alongside Dove's more formal clothes and a fur stole, none of which she'd worn for years. The wardrobe smelled very faintly of verbena and suddenly Dove was five years old again, listening to Verena and Maisie talking somewhere out of sight; seeing only the black, shiny hem of a dress showing above satin shoes fastened with a sparkling buckle. As soon as they became aware of Dove hiding under the bed, the talking had stopped and Maisie had taken Dove's hand, laughing as they went downstairs to find sponge fingers to have as a treat with her bedtime milk.

Dove had looked around for the pearls and she saw them lying in an iridescent, anguine curve in the dusting of talcum powder on her dressing table. She had put out a hand as if she expected the beads to move, to detain them from slithering away, but they lay in a sinuous rope until Dove snatched them up and threw them into the back of the wardrobe, contaminated by what she had so abruptly understood.

Dove told Lewis only that Sylvie had been unsatisfactory and she found a younger girl to take her place. Maisie, of course, was not deceived: she tried to talk to Dove, to limit her distress, but Dove listened to her mother with no indulgence at all. The thought of her beloved grandfather, Matabele Jack, and Gracie Beckerleg, whom she had always regarded as the more unprepossessing of the sisters, together producing the woman whom Dove had seen reflected in the glass, a woman with Dove's own features, wearing Dove's own clothes, made her feel sullied and defiled as if some legacy of licentiousness had been passed on to her: a failing, some frailty which she knew that she must guard against as it might threaten to overwhelm her and could yet prove to be more than she was able to contain.

Maisie was as untroubled by the thought of her father's infidelity as she was, much later, by Pender's peccadilloes but she accepted that Dove was different and had, she now understood, no way of reconciling what she remembered of her grandfather with the evidence of his betrayal of Verena.

In time Dove consigned Sylvie Beckerleg to a part of her mind where, like the pearls in the wardrobe, she was rejected as unworthy of consideration. Maisie's infrequent contact with Sylvie was accepted by the Beckerlegs as no more than could be expected although they had, from time to time, found it opportune to be connected to a family which was in a position to help them financially at times when there had been a shortfall between the income from the little shop and what they needed to live on.

There was an understanding between the Beckerleg sisters and Maisie Eustace: her help was discreet and had been mutually sustaining for many years. It was a legacy which Dove would have inherited had she been more tolerant in her acceptance of their compromise.

After lunch Dove had suggested that Maisie might like to come into the garden with her. 'Every time I look out of the window I remember that I've been meaning to tidy up the beds round the house and it's such a lovely day you could sit and watch for a bit if you wrap up warmly. Would you like to do that?'

What Maisie really wanted to do was to watch television while she crocheted but she would never have told Dove this, so she fetched her violet cashmere shawl and followed Dove into the passage which led to the back door. The floor was of old red tiles and she watched her feet in their new bronze shoes in case she tripped on an uneven edge. Dove pulled on a pair of wellington boots and reached for a man's old, thick cardigan which one of the girls had bought at a jumble sale. The elbows were patched with Liberty remnants and there was a hole in the front where a pruned branch had taken revenge and caught the wool, tearing it open.

Dove did her hair in the morning, subjugating the almost uncontrollable curls and waves into a chignon, after which she scarcely looked at it again all day. She didn't bother to do so now and Maisie thought it a shame that Dove had adopted such a severe style: she put out a hand, as she had done when her daughter was a little girl, to touch the thick coils of hair like gold wire which had always been Dove's most striking feature.

Dove had fetched a large plastic sheet which she spread out on the cobbled path to collect twigs and dead stalks as she worked her way along the narrow beds which bordered the walls of the house. She had been working for about half an hour, talking intermittently to Maisie, who had become bored and was wondering how soon she could convincingly plead that she was feeling the cold and could retreat into her afternoon programmes, when Lawry's car had arrived.

Dove found these days that she needed to pace herself, to rest her back from time to time, and when the car had driven up she had been having a break from her rhythmic progress along the side of the house. She had walked with Maisie to a point about a hundred yards down the garden to see whether the Christmas roses were already showing through the earth and from there they were screened by a stand of zigzag bamboo, dense camouflage, allowing covert speculation about the man and woman who turned the corner of the house and stood together, arm in arm looking around the garden.

Maisie's boredom vanished instantly. 'Who ever's that with Lawry, do you suppose? Even he can't have abandoned the bride already can he, because that's not the woman in the photo. This one looks too old and not at all glamorous. Not a bit his type.'

'Hush, Mother, they'll hear you, but you're right, she's no child bride, is she?' Dove was about to step from behind the bamboo but hesitated, as curious as her mother about

Lawry's companion. She was certainly not a girl, dressed in a jacket and skirt neither brown nor grey, but which reminded Dove of mouse's fur. Her shoes were black, flat and fastened over the instep with a wide strap and a buckle. The woman's hair was brown, neither dark nor fair, and neither short nor long, but resting lightly on the back of her neck. She was smiling and even from her place of concealment Dove could see that she had good teeth.

'Mother! Dove! We're here. We've arrived.'

Dove stepped out from behind the bamboo, making a good job of feigning surprise and pulling off two odd gloves of Lewis's that she wore for gardening. As she walked towards the couple Dove was aware of Loretta watching her, the smile still on her face, hazel eyes observant. At once Dove became aware of how peculiar she must look to a stranger, conscious of the patched and torn cardigan and her untidy hair. She didn't mind about them particularly but she did feel disadvantaged by the odd shuffle at which she had to approach her new sister-in-law. Dove was wearing Lewis's boots: annoyed that one of the girls must have borrowed hers and too impatient to try and find them, Dove had slipped on the nearest pair she could lay her hands on: Lewis's, and three sizes too big for her.

Now she hobbled and clumped her way across the grass to kiss her brother and to wonder how she should greet his wife; she certainly had no intention of kissing her and held out her hand, uncomfortably certain that Loretta had been well aware of Maisie and Dove's scrutiny from behind the bamboo. As soon as it was possible to do so, Dove left them and shambled into the house to change into her shoes, nearly tripping over a pile of suitcases and bags just inside the back door. She stood aside as Maisie drove her small flock into Dove's kitchen; Lawry unaware of his sister's resentment, Loretta mindful enough for both of them;

conciliatory, apologetic for arriving a day early and for not letting Dove know.

The kitchen smelled of nutmeg and cinnamon, the cake that Dove had made for their tea tomorrow standing on a wire cooling tray. She laid the back of her hand on the top of it, fruit and cherries surfacing the shiny crust in perfect alignment like cobbles in a dark street. 'I don't know if it's cold enough to cut yet, I only made it this morning. Do sit down and I'll make tea.'

Loretta looked around the kitchen which was not altogether as she had expected it to be. It was large, more than slightly shabby and full of the kind of china and utensils which she would have bought piecemeal as jumble or sought out at car boot sales, and she was surprised to notice at once that nothing looked new. The air of practical simplicity was uncontrived, a large Welsh dresser along one wall supporting serviceable equipment, used every day and purposeful, Dove preferring the furniture which Maisie had taken over from Verena to something more modern and fitted.

There was a wooden table in the middle of the room with six or seven chairs around it, unmatched, except that all of them resembled the table in their sturdy plain frames. Loretta, used to kitchens where a washing machine and refrigerator dictated the use of the rest of the available space, was puzzled for a moment that Dove seemed to have neither but when Dove walked into a separate pantry to fetch milk for their tea, she realised that there were rooms and cupboards unseen that opened off the kitchen and where, she supposed, were housed those necessities whose absence she had noticed.

That Rejerrah was a bigger house than Loretta had antici- pated had been obvious as soon as Lawry had driven in through the open gates, but that it was little changed since Verena and Jack Woodvine had lived there, came as a surprise. It wasn't that she was unused to the principle of thrift; she had grown up with the knowledge that profligacy was not to be encouraged, and in a household such as her parents had achieved, there was no waste and very little to spare. Here, at Rejerrah, in Lawry's boyhood home, Loretta experienced for the first time the ordered pattern of a family who had established from the first their appointed way of life and who had seen little reason to change it.

It was, Loretta Eustace had yet to learn, a family where women had for many years prevailed; the men they married almost inconsequential to the continuation of the way life at Rejerrah was ordered.

5

'Dove's a very unusual name.'

'Is it? I've never considered it so. More than Loretta, would you say?'

'Well, I've known other Lorettas – there were two more in my year at school – but never another Dove.'

'What about Paloma Picasso?' Loretta looked blank. 'Paloma is Spanish for Dove.' Loretta still seemed not to understand so Dove said no more but as the silence lengthened, she relented and went on, 'Actually, I wasn't named after the bird at all: my parents made up my name from the first two letters of the names of my grandmothers. One was named Dolly Eustace and the other Verena Woodvine. So, DO . . . VE.'

Loretta mulled this over. 'What about Lawry? Until we got married and I heard his full name for the first time, I'd always assumed that his name was Lawrence.'

'He was named after a friend of our father's, Trenerry Lawry who, in turn, took his name from his mother's maiden name. Or so I believe.' Dove was smearing fat over a leg of pork. She worked it into every curve and wrinkle of the skin as conscientiously as a beautician giving a facial, her fingers sliding and slithering over the pallid flesh. She looked sideways at Loretta before moving to the sink to wash her hands. When most of the grease had been dispersed, Dove returned to the meat and sprinkled it thickly with salt, repeating her kneading and massaging until a crust of crystals covered the fat. 'That should do it.'

'Do what?'

'Make good crackling: a little fat, lots of salt and a hot oven. Don't you cook, Loretta?'

'Yes, I do. I'm quite good at it actually and my pastry's particularly nice.' Loretta watched Dove wash her hands again, this time making sure all trace of grease and salt was gone, cleaning her fingernails with a file which she took from a green glass vase on the dresser. Loretta turned her head away from the sight of the pork, shaking it slightly as if to dislodge any thought hiding, uncalled for, in her mind.

Dove made a face. 'Messy, but the only way.' She slid the meat in its pan into the oven. 'Would you like to put the kettle on, please, while I tidy up?'

'What did you say your father's friend was called?' Loretta filled the kettle and plugged it in.

'Trenerry Lawry.'

'So why wasn't Lawry called Trenerry?'

Dove looked at Loretta with detachment, at her colourless hair and pale eyes set in shadowy brown sockets: Dove thought the question was hardly worthy of consideration but Loretta said again, 'Why did your father call him Lawry?'

Dove was suddenly impatient. 'I've never bothered to think about it much, but I believe it's quite usual in Cornwall to use a surname for a first name.'

'Like your uncle Pender? That's another odd name – Pender.'

'You think so? His older brother, who died in the war, was called Grenfell. Both family names. Does it matter?'

'I like to understand these things.'

'I see.'

'And I've never come across anyone calling their mother

by her Christian name the way you and Lawry do. Didn't you call her mummy even when you were small?'

Dove thought about this for a moment. 'I can't remember ever calling her anything other than Maisie when we were young: perhaps it was because we didn't have a father around for very long, so instead of a mummy and daddy we just had Maisie.' Anticipating Loretta's next question Dove asked, 'Do you want to know where that name came from as well?' Loretta nodded and Dove went on, 'Maisie's father was always known as Matabele Jack Woodvine because he did rather tend to start a conversation by saying, "When I was in Matabeleland". It became a family joke but he actually had lived there as a young man, as well as in South Africa, so when he married Verena, my grandmother, and they had a daughter in between the two boys, Matabele Jack used to refer to her as "my little *meisie*". *Meisie* is Afrikaans for girl, you see, and after a while everyone copied him, and she became known as Maisie.' Dove didn't really want to discuss her family with Loretta and hoped that such small information would satisfy her curiosity for a while.

Dove found Loretta's constant attendance on her oppressive. Each time she tried to escape to the kitchen, Loretta would follow, talking incessantly, asking what she could do to help. Now Dove directed her to the sack of potatoes in the pantry and watched, exasperated, as Loretta filled a bowl, working methodically and steadily until Dove took over, hands swift and capable.

'You'll never get all those around the meat, will you?' Loretta said and Dove had forced herself to reply civilly that, no, actually she was planning on using a separate roasting pan. Loretta seemed to examine this as if it were important, before asking Dove what job she could do next.

Dove suggested that Loretta make coffee and stopped, appalled, hearing herself talking in the voice she used to direct the providers of refreshment and the stall holders at

St John Bosco when she went with Maisie to help at the summer and Christmas bazaars. Dove made an effort and smiled at her sister-in-law. 'I'm so used to cooking for a lot of people that it's really not an effort for me, so why don't you just sit and talk to me while I do the vegetables.'

Loretta pulled a chair out from under the kitchen table and scrutinised it hard in the way that was becoming familiar to Dove before sitting down, watching Dove peeling and chopping two swedes and washing what seemed like an unbelievably large Savoy cabbage. Dove glanced at her and laughed, genuinely amused at the look on Loretta's face. 'We'll eat all this and someone is sure to say that there are never enough roast potatoes. They always do, you'll see.'

'Don't you mind?'

'Mind what?' Dove was surprised by the question. 'All the cooking, do you mean?' Loretta nodded and Dove looked at the cabbage on the chopping board. She felt it, like bubble wrap but veined, blue and waxy under her fingers. Loretta's voice had been concerned as if the answer to the foolish question was of positive interest to her, and for a moment Dove wanted to turn to her and say, 'Of course I mind: I mind that no one even considers that I might prefer to be reading a book somewhere quiet on my own, or walking by the sea, or doing nothing. Just *not* doing anything for a change.' Dove struggled to master her breathing, to sound matter of fact, dismissive, but was astonished to find herself on the verge of tears. She concentrated on shredding the cabbage into fine, regular strips, determined not to cry in front of her brother's discomfiting new wife.

When she had regained control of her voice, Dove said, 'I don't really think about it: it's just something I have to do, so I do it. It's like any other job I suppose.'

'Except that there's no job description, no statutory hours and no paid overtime.'

Dove was exasperated now. 'Perhaps I should appoint

you as my union representative and you could negotiate a good deal for me.'

'I could certainly negotiate a better deal for you.' Dove looked at Loretta and was astonished to see that the other woman was perfectly serious.

'A bit late for all that, don't you think, and, besides, what else should I do? I've spent thirty years looking after other people. It's the one thing I *can* do.'

'You can do whatever you want to do. Or at least you can try to.' Loretta's eyes were fixed on Dove and Dove felt feeble and diminished as if thirty years of unselfish devotion had left her expendable in Loretta's eyes.

'What about my mother? She needs me. If I were off somewhere following my own inclinations as you suggest, what would happen to her?'

'She could go and live in a retirement home; I expect she could afford to couldn't she? And you could visit her when it suited you and not have to organise your day around her.'

'But I *like* having Maisie next door. I enjoy looking after her, and Pender too, if it comes to that.' Although she tried to sound light-hearted, Dove was angry. She resented the intrusion of Loretta's words, disconcerting and dangerous as they were, into areas which were personal and particular. Dove looked with sudden deep dislike at the slight figure dressed today, not in the mouse-shaded clothes in which she had arrived, but in a skirt and cardigan the colour of porridge, relieved only by a thin gold chain from which hung a cross. A second, longer, chain carried the initials LE in curly letters and Dove could only suppose that Lawry must have given this to Loretta after they were married. Dove's hand went almost unconsciously to her throat where she wore, as always, the pearls Maisie had given her when she was twenty-one, and she smiled to herself, knowing that Loretta would never understand the difference. The thought restored Dove somewhat and she reminded Loretta that the kettle had boiled and that as Maisie and Pender were joining them, there would be eight people for coffee.

As soon as she had poured water into the filter Loretta sat down once more and watched Dove closely, following her movements as if to etch them on her memory. 'I never realised that Lawry's home was so big,' she said, 'he didn't say.'

'Lawry's home?'

'This house. Rejerrah. How many bedrooms are there – about six?'

'About that.' Dove was discovering that Loretta didn't expect conversation; a word or two was enough to keep her primed. 'More, if you count Maisie's and Pender's and the attics, which we don't use.'

'When he told me about his home in Cornwall I didn't expect anything like this. I thought it would be . . .'

'Just a moment,' Dove's voice was very quiet. 'What gives you the idea that Rejerrah is Lawry's home? Rejerrah is *my* home, and my husband's and my daughters'. It is also my mother's home and her brother's, but it hasn't been Lawry's home for many years, nor will it be ever again.'

'But he said . . .'

'Listen, Loretta,' Dove was determined that her sister-in-law should understand the position. 'When you've been married to my brother for a little while longer, you'll discover that he says a lot of things that aren't absolutely accurate.'

'But he thinks of it as his home.'

'Then he is incorrect.'

'But Dove,' Loretta looked like a child who has chosen the wrong hand hidden behind an adult's back. 'Is it fair that you should have this house and everything that goes with it; the huge garden, I mean, and the flat and all the other bits, when poor Lawry hasn't got anything?'

'Look, I think perhaps there's something that "poor Lawry", as you call him, must have forgotten to tell you: when Maisie made Rejerrah over to me, she gave the exact value of everything to Lawry. He wanted the money to start his first business and if he hadn't lost the lot, it would probably be worth much more than Rejerrah is now. It was, and is, a perfectly fair arrangement.'

Dove looked at Loretta to see if she understood. At times she seemed not to follow what was being said to her, but Dove was beginning to realise that with the odd concentration with which her sister-in-law watched and listened to everything around her, she missed very little. Now Loretta said nothing and Dove fetched her notebook from the dresser, crossing off all the jobs she had accomplished that morning. She chose a thick, felt-tipped pen and enjoyed watching the inky obliteration of those tasks which she had found tedious but inescapable.

'Shall I take their coffee to the others?' Loretta asked and Dove directed her into the drawing room, escaping with her own mug to the bedroom. There, she took off the old shirt and jeans which she had put on when she had first got up, and lay on the bed, irritable and unsettled.

Everything that Loretta had said Dove wanted to dismiss as the prattling of a thoughtless child. It was as if Loretta gave no thought at all to the consequences of her words but there was, in even the shallowest of her observations, the truth that someone more constrained would hesitate to speak. Dove knew that she had thought of a life without Maisie and Pender to look after; a life where she could do as she pleased, come and go unremarked and unobserved; spend money without the thought that it had been noted and commented upon. The rush of tears that had followed Loretta's concern at Dove having to cook for so many people all the time had unnerved her, because the truth was that she no longer enjoyed doing it. What had been a pleasure for so long had become merely another chore – but that was something which Dove would never admit.

She thought of the years when the house had always been full of her daughters' friends; when she never knew how many people were going to sit down at the table to be fed and of how much she had enjoyed being the centre around which life at Rejerrah had revolved. She had never thought ahead to a time when it would end and now Dove had a sudden, saddening realisation that she hadn't picked blackberries this autumn because there was still last year's bramble jelly left in the pantry and no one to eat it.

Perhaps this is what getting old is, Dove thought: that there is no longer the necessity to do what you have always done, that what was once so vital is no longer even important. Dove wondered if that was what was wrong with Lewis but knew that it wasn't so. Perhaps, she thought, it is only me who is no longer important, perhaps I have become peripheral to his life and Lewis has understood that much sooner than I have done.

Dove didn't feel able to think about Lewis just now; she had the beginning of a headache and searched in the drawer of the bedside table for paracetamol, swallowing two capsules with the last of her cold coffee. The house was very quiet, with the dull contentment of a Sunday morning spent reading the newspapers after a more elaborate than usual breakfast. Pender had taken Maisie to early Mass at St John Bosco and Maisie, returning, had complained that the visiting priest had preached a sermon incomprehensible to her, about civil war in Africa. There was no longer a resident priest in Penalverne and the level of pastoral care in the parish was variable and unreliable. Only habit and a certain tenacity of faith enabled Maisie to continue in her regular worship. Pender accompanied her simply as her escort.

Dove lay on her bed a while longer. She would have liked to have crept under the covers and tried to sleep but once her headache had receded a little she undressed and went into the bathroom to shower, the warm water on the back of her neck often alleviating the pain in her head.

Dove knew that she should make an effort to make this Sunday special, to welcome her brother and his new wife to Rejerrah. She opened the wardrobe that had once belonged to Verena and which now sheltered her own clothes, lost in its cavernous, verbena-scented depths. There were two hanging cupboards and in between them there were shelves and drawers in which Dove's modest accumulation of clothes lay, scarcely disturbing the space.

Choosing what to wear had become a problem; Dove had reached an age where she was afraid of looking ridiculous – mutton dressed as lamb – or worse still, set forever in the mould of her girlhood where Grace Kelly and Jackie Kennedy had been the ideal to which everyone had aspired. On the other hand, permed hair and wide shoes seemed such an admission of middle age that Dove felt bound to try to find an acceptable alternative. She looked at the navy blue and forest green, relieved here and there by a modest violet, hanging uninvitingly in front of her. Sometimes nothing at all looked right and Dove chose, as she usually did, a floral skirt and a well-ironed shirt, wishing she had the insouciance to dress like Bethan in layers of black jersey and to wear little pointed boots which reminded Dove of the witch in the *Wizard of Oz*.

Dove went downstairs determined to avoid Loretta if she possibly could, thinking that it was time for Maisie to take a turn at entertaining the child bride.

'Delicious, Dove my dear, as always.' Pender wiped his mouth on one of the big white napkins which Dove always set out for Sunday lunch. He gave her one of his Maurice Chevalier smiles, intimate, suggestive that he, more than anyone around the table, appreciated the excellence of her cooking. 'Only one small criticism, if you will allow me.'

Diana and Jossy exchanged a look, put down their knives and forks and chanted together, 'Not *quite* enough roast potatoes.'

Dove joined in the ritual laughter, looking to see if Loretta remembered what she had been told in the kitchen. Dove was disconcerted and had to hide a smile as Loretta turned towards Pender and said, 'Oh, do you really think so, Pender? I thought there were plenty to go round and Dove did try to make sure there were enough. Look, there's even a small one left in the dish.'

There was a delighted silence and Dove wondered if Lawry would try to explain: she did hope that he wouldn't. Pender cleared his throat and tried to avoid Maisie's questing eye. The two girls picked up empty serving dishes and Dove could hear muffled laughter as they scuffled together down the passage to the kitchen, any animosity forgotten in shared enjoyment of the moment.

Lunch had been a series of excursions into unfamiliar territory, sorties from base camp of the known and the customary. Maisie had dribbled gravy down the front of her dress as she did every Sunday; Lewis had entertained Lawry and his new wife with what his daughters called Tales from the Valleys, and Pender had kept up a gentle undertow of gossip.

It had all been so perfectly ordinary: the well-known jokes, the familiar enquiries requiring no real answer; even Lewis's stories, new to Loretta, were known word-perfect to those who had heard them before. The food they had eaten was that which Dove always cooked when they were together: the pork had been followed by a pudding, known to them all for some reason long forgotten, as the Queen Mother's Favourite. It was sticky and rich and even Diana had asked for a second helping.

She and Jossy had volunteered to clear up and they had brought fresh coffee into the dining room where the others sat, satisfied and too languorous to think of moving. Dove passed the small cups around, knowing what everyone except Loretta would need, sweeteners or sugar and cream. Maisie's contribution to the lunch had been a box of peppermint creams and as Dove reached into the middle of the table for one she heard Pender ask Lawry if he and Loretta had plans for the next few days.

'I only ask,' he said, 'because I believe the weather is changing and if you want to do the Zennor coast drive, I'd advise sooner rather than later. At this time of the year it does tend to set in, rather.'

Dove looked towards her uncle but was diverted by the sight of Loretta choosing a peppermint cream. Women have a special way of holding things as if, by the exact placement of a hand, the intrinsic value of an object is enhanced, and Loretta was holding the sweet in its green, bark-textured foil as if it were precious, an amulet resting on the palm of her hand. She unwrapped it very gently and smoothed the foil over and over again until the pattern was evened out, the edges curling upwards a little, like small, half formed waves. Then Loretta ate the peppermint cream and when she had finished, and wiped her mouth, she turned to Pender, pale eyes seeking his before she spoke.

'Lawry said he'd take me to Zennor but there's no rush is there? There are so many places I'd like to see but we've got lots of time, haven't we, Lawry?'

Dove, alerted, looked at her sister-in-law. 'I'd say that rather depends: what would *you* say, Lawry? *Have* you plenty of time? After all, you haven't told us anything about your job yet, or where you're going to live now that you're married, because I don't suppose your flat will be big enough for two, will it?'

Lawry laced his fingers together, stretching his arms so

that the knuckles cracked. He tried a smile. 'As you say, that depends. Depends on how long you can put up with us.'

Loretta reached for another peppermint cream and Dove watched her once more smoothing and flattening the foil before she allowed herself to put the sweet into her mouth. Maisie, who hadn't really been listening to the conversation suddenly became aware that the atmosphere had changed and looked from Dove to Pender, hoping for some sort of sign as to what had happened while she had been distracted, trying to avoid yielding to sleep.

Lawry smiled at his mother, speaking rather too loudly as if she were deaf. 'Just saying, Maisie, we wonder how long you can all put up with us. Or put us up, if you want to put it another way.'

'Lawry said.' In the silence that followed this statement everyone at the table turned towards Loretta. 'Lawry said,' she started again, 'that as you've got so much room here, perhaps we could stay until he finds a new job and somewhere for us to live.'

The wallpaper in the dining room at Rejerrah was cream, satin fleur-de-lys on a background of plain and embossed stripes. It had been in the house for a very long time and there was a patch over the serving table where grease from the turkey had erupted the Christmas before Verena had died. It had left a mark which was an approximation of the north island of New Zealand. Now Dove looked at the stain as if she had only just noticed it, letting her eyes trace the outline of the coast from Whangarei to Wellington. She lingered in the Bay of Plenty and forced herself to pause again at the Cook Strait, before travelling up past Auckland to the North Cape. She was too angry to speak and only Lawry's wife was unaware of it.

Loretta looked closely at Dove, following her gaze to the mark on the wall. 'You could get that out, you know, if you used brown paper and a hot iron. You iron over the paper and it absorbs the grease.'

'Thank you for that handy hint, I'll certainly bear it in mind.' Dove's voice was ominously controlled and Lewis glanced at Pender but Pender bent swiftly to retrieve his napkin which, quite deliberately, he had allowed to fall to the floor. Dove lowered her head: from the corner of her eye she could see Maisie, the expressionless immobility of her mother reflecting Dove's own realisation that Loretta was a terrible mistake.

'Always rely on Loretta for the direct approach.' Lawry tried to sound buoyant but there was no response from anyone so he went on, 'Actually, what I thought was; well, what I hoped was, that we could use the flat over the garage. It wouldn't be for long, just until we get ourselves straight.'

Pender crossed his legs, admiring the yellow socks that showed just enough under his black-and-white-checked trousers. 'Are we to understand then, dear boy, that you have no job, nor anywhere to live?'

Dove waited; a thin, whippy branch of winter jasmine scratched at the window, yellow flowers the colour of Pender's socks starred along its length. Little bursts of talk came from the kitchen and a sudden silence following the tinkle of broken glass before laughter and the slurring sound that Dove knew must be one of the girls sweeping up the shards. Dove wondered why it was never the cheap, easily replaced glasses that broke and was prepared for a shame-faced Jossy or an unconcerned Diana to tell her that another of Verena's crystals had gone.

Pender was speaking again. 'I'm afraid, Lawry, that you've been pipped at the post for the flat: friend of mine's moving in next week as a matter of fact. She's in a bit of a tight spot and we're just waiting for Dove's final say so before she moves her things across.' Pender had long, beautiful hands and he rested one on the table, crumpling his napkin, smooth square nails slightly shiny like a woman's. 'Right, Dove?' His smile was full of complicity.

Dove, caught between her brother's assumption and her uncle's perfidious solution, looked at Pender. 'I thought we'd already agreed that Mrs Fielding would move in next week.' She had no need to ask who Pender's unnamed friend would be and she missed entirely the way Lewis reacted to her words, hiding his gratification by fussing with the coffee pot, smiling at Maisie as he insisted on refilling her cup, pushing the peppermint creams towards Loretta.

'Any chance of us staying in the house then?'

'What?' Dove had forgotten Lawry as she struggled to come to terms with the way Pender had manipulated her. She supposed that he must be telling the truth and she suspected that Lewis had known of her uncle's duplicity. Dove glanced at Lewis but he was studying the list of contents printed in gold on the dark green carton which still held a few mints. 'What did you say, Lawry?'

'I wondered if there's any chance of us staying on here for a while?'

Dove looked at her brother; a face that was saved from dissolution by a disappointed mouth and innocent eyes, and she nearly surrendered. It was Loretta, sitting watching Dove, certain in her complacency, who made the refusal easy. Loretta's face remained expressionless but Lawry laughed. It wasn't mirthful but accepting of what he had known Dove's answer would be.

Lewis spoke, his voice sounding very loud in the subdued air of the dining room. 'This time of the year, there are always places to rent – holiday lets empty for the winter. You should find somewhere without too much difficulty. Sorry we can't help.'

'But Pender's friend wouldn't be coming here if she'd

been able to find somewhere else would she?' Dove looked at Loretta with distaste.

'Didn't say that.' Pender uncrossed his legs, crossing them again with the other knee uppermost. He felt in desperate need of a cigarette but with Dove in her present mood he thought better of it. He was quite unfazed by Loretta. 'Only said she was in a bit of a tight spot. I don't think it's for me to enlarge on the details but it touches on a violent husband, divorce – you know the sort of thing. We thought,' he said, changing it hurriedly to, '*I* thought, she'd be safer where other people could keep an eye on her and the children.'

'I'd forgotten the children. How many are there?' asked Dove, resentment at the position in which she found herself threatening to overwhelm caution.

'Two,' said Lewis and Pender together, Pender adding, 'Cody and Freya.'

'And how old are Cody and Freya? And what sex, for goodness' sake, is Cody?'

'Male, and he's seven; Freya's nine.'

There seemed nothing more to say and Dove, sighing, started gathering used napkins to put in the washing machine, her well intentioned luncheon now no more than an assembly of hurt feelings and misunderstandings. She avoided Maisie's eye and dropped the pile of white linen onto a chair in the passage before taking the old cardigan off its peg and letting herself out into the garden.

The tiles underfoot in the kitchen passage had been clammy, always a sign of dampness in the air, but outside in the garden Dove was surprised at the freshness of the afternoon. There were high clouds scudding inland but the wind was mild and Dove could have imagined that it was almost spring. Instead of going into the garden as she had intended, she turned out of the gate and walked along under the wall of Rejerrah where it bordered the main road. Just for a little while Dove wanted to be far away from her family, feeling heavy and tired, encumbered by the complications of other people's lives. And her headache was returning.

For most of her life Dove had been an observer, a translator of disturbance into tranquillity; composure replacing agitation in a child's mind, or a friend's apprehension turning into acceptance under Dove's realistic assessment of a situation. No one went to Dove for a facile solution to a problem or with the certainty of being cheered but Dove listened carefully, and out of the welter of words she selected those which enabled her to understand what was really being said. Her advice was pragmatic but not intrusive and she never spoke of what she knew.

'The thing about Dove Courtney,' people said, 'is that she is so *sensible*, so reliable and down to earth.' Most people who knew Dove respected her, some even admired her worthiness, but Dove would have settled for love of the kind she saw so clearly between Maisie and her friends but which, Dove knew, had eluded her. She was honest enough to acknowledge her loss.

Lewis had loved Dove once, and perhaps still did, but it was a staid, convenient fondness and Dove longed sometimes for the excitement which she knew would never come again. Why hadn't she known at the time that she needed to capture and treasure love, to save it, just as she had encouraged her daughters to put their pennies away for a rainy day. Every day seemed to have its share of rain now and there was so little saved on which she could draw: too much activity a refuge where Dove could shelter from bewilderment at the discontent she felt for a life she no longer seemed able to recognise as her own.

In the shelter of the wall Dove was warm enough and walked as far as the roundabout where the roads separated into those familiar and often used and those which led to the coast and were associated in Dove's mind with treats:

picnics with the children on empty, hidden beaches; pasties eaten in a pub garden about which she never told Lewis; or sitting in the car by Ding Dong Mine eating saffron buns from a paper bag, bought earlier when she had been in St Just. The island in the middle of the roundabout still bore flowers which, from a distance, looked thriving and colourful but when Dove got nearer she stopped to look more closely and realised that nothing in the tightly planted beds was perfect any more.

There was mud on the road, still slick and sticky from the earlier rain, Dove careful to avoid it in her unsuitable Sunday shoes. A car passed her, tooting gently as a warning, and she realised that she was standing in the road and moved back to the safety of the pavement. The island bed was full of agaves, the tips of the sword-shaped leaves ragged and torn by many gales. The flame-coloured canna lilies were still bright, but shabby like a favourite, worn out dress; and pink and bronze begonias, which reminded Dove of an old fox fur of Maisie's, curled around the shoulders of the bed, enclosing marigolds and heliotrope long after they should have been dug up and replaced by tulip bulbs and the stiff rosettes of primula ready to divert the eye in spring.

Beyond the roundabout the road rose slightly and then dropped away, leaving palm trees and pines silhouetted against the sky. They looked suddenly sinister and Dove realised that the sky was changing to a sulphurous yellow which she knew meant rain. Dove loved rain and had always longed to be in India when the monsoon broke or to visit Cherrapunji to see it for herself, but Cornwall in November was a different matter and reluctantly she turned back towards Rejerrah. It was time, Dove thought, for one of her little holidays.

6

'Maisie?'

'Yes, darling.'

'While Diana's here to keep an eye on you I thought I might have a little holiday. How would you feel about that?'

'I think you should, Dove. You've been looking awfully peaky lately – even Pender noticed. Lewis doesn't mind?'

'Haven't asked him yet.'

Maisie was thinking of going to bed and Dove had come around, as she did each evening, to see her mother safely settled for the night. A glass of water was on the bedside table, Maisie's glasses and her prayer book next to it. She slept fitfully and often read for a while in the night, or lay thinking, mainly of long ago and people who had been her friends.

'Maisie?' Dove spoke again, stroking the cushion she was holding, appliquéd auriculas in pots on a dark green background, which Bethan had found for her grandmother in a car boot sale and with which she had parted reluctantly.

'If something's worrying you, why don't you tell me what it is?'

'It sounds so silly.'

'Not silly at all if it's upsetting you.'

The words were light like moths and they fluttered and

settled on Maisie's shawl thrown over the sofa, and the embroidered footstool in front of her chair, coming to rest on her shoulders, wings folded and powdery and fragile. Dove impaled them on the silver pins of her words. 'I'm afraid of getting old.'

She waited for her mother's laugh so that she could join in and banish from her mind thoughts she knew to be illogical, but Maisie didn't laugh, only leaned her head back against the crocheted square on her chair and closed her eyes. Dove looked at her and wondered how two women who had shared one body could be so different. Maisie sighed and opening her eyes again, turned her head to look at Dove. 'Well, as someone once said, it's better than the alternative, wouldn't you say?'

'Is it? Is it really, Maisie?'

Maisie was startled: had she failed her daughter so profoundly that Dove considered old age to be no more than decrepitude and loss? Maisie had watched Girlie Eustace struggling with an unavailing body and knew that her life was good: and Enid, too, in late middle age had found a way to live that gave her satisfaction and for which she was grateful. Maisie never questioned the desirability of getting old; it had been so gradual a process that she scarcely recognised it and even now she would describe herself as merely elderly – old was not for another ten years at least.

'Tell me what's good about it.'

'Well, it doesn't matter if people think that you're bonkers because if you are, you probably don't know it. And – let me think – I know! You can wear comfortable things like socks and old cardigans in bed, and dreadful hats indoors.' Maisie, determined to present a cheerful picture to Dove, looked at her. 'I bet even you didn't know that I sometimes wear a hat in the house – just when it's a bit draughty in the kitchen.'

'Oh Maisie, why didn't you tell me that it's draughty? I'll get someone to have a look at it. Probably the window.'

'That's what I mean, Dove. I *like* wearing a hat indoors, but that's because I'm old and I probably *am* bonkers. You immediately think of repairing whatever is defective, and that's because you're neither.'

'Is that all? Isn't there anything else besides socks and hats and cardigans?' Dove's voice was bleak and Maisie looked at her for a long time, trying to see again the little girl with burning golden hair and a laugh like the gurgle of pouring wine.

'I've built up a family that I love and whom, I believe, loves me: I still have a brother and when I'm with him I can be a child again, that doesn't change.' Maisie didn't tell Dove how often she thought of the two young men killed in the war, her husband and her older brother, but went on, 'Then there are friends; dear friends, old friends who are so different from new friends. You see, Dove, I don't know what it's like to be old because I don't believe that I am. In my head I'm still as young as I ever was; it's just that now I know a bit more and worry a bit less.'

'But your body, Maisie, the bits that don't work as well as they did, doesn't that make you upset?' Dove's voice was tentative, as if it held some knowledge of trespass. 'I'm afraid, you see, that I'll turn into one of those old women you hope you don't have to stand behind in the queue at the post office.'

Maisie thought for a minute. 'I suppose something happening suddenly is worse, like Girlie's stroke, because you don't have time to get used to it. The rest just creeps up on you and becomes familiar and accepted.'

'I suppose so.' Dove put the cushion back on her uncle's chair. 'Age doesn't seem to have slowed Pender down very much, does it? Is he being foolish, Maisie, is Anita Fielding going to be a problem? I don't think I can stand her and Loretta at the same time, not a coherent thought between them.'

'You're wrong there, Dove, plenty of coherent thoughts I fancy, just not very . . .'

Dove became aware of a terrible smell seeping into the room and looked in alarm towards her mother. Maisie seemed unaware of any disruption and it was only a groan and the creaking of a basket that reminded Dove of Sandy's presence under Pender's desk. She laughed and Maisie looked at her, not understanding Dove's change of mood. 'Sandy's made the most horrible fart and you didn't even notice, did you?'

'Well, there you are: it's one of the big, big advantages of being old, one's sense of smell diminishing so.'

'How *can* that be an advantage, Maisie? There must be so much that you miss.'

'Ah, but you see, imagination takes over. When one of your darling girls brings me flowers, I remember the stephanotis that I had in my wedding bouquet, and freesias and those yellow azaleas that smell of honey, and I can be anywhere at all in my mind.' Maisie's speckled hands, so like Pender's, lay quietly along the arms of the chair. 'I can still smell most things; bacon and melon and Blue Grass, but it's all muted and bound up so in memory.

'I see grass drying in the sun and sometimes I wonder whether that musty sweetness is truly here in England, in Cornwall, at all. Perhaps it's hay lying in the fields long ago in Africa when it was dry even before it was cut. Sometimes,' she closed her eyes, 'I imagine we're back on the farm where everything was dry, dry as dust, and the earth was red and the smells were different altogether.'

Maisie's voice stopped, Dove watching her mother's face soften as she thought of her childhood with Verena and Matabele Jack and her two brothers. Maisie looked at Dove and smiled. 'It means, you see, that piddle and the decay that is so embarrassing when one is only *becoming* old, isn't very intrusive any more. One is able to accept it in others and just hope that they will accept it in you.'

Dove leaned forward and kissed her mother's criss-crossed cheek. 'I hope I'm as kind as you when I'm your age.'

'You're kinder than me now: much *too* kind to the attendant poor.'

'Mother!'

'You see, I'm not kind at all. I needn't have said that.'

'You mean Lawry and Loretta? God, they sound like a country music duo; Cornwall's answer to Conway Twitty and Loretta Lynn.'

'Possibly: or Anita Fielding, she's another one whose situation is provoking, wouldn't you say?' Maisie watched Dove for her reaction but there was nothing more than amused exasperation at the thought of Pender's foolhardiness. Dove, then, thought Maisie, was unaware of Lewis's interest in Anita Fielding: perhaps it could be contained, perhaps Dove need never know, but Maisie was unconvinced that this would be so.

She changed the subject, 'Where are you thinking of going this time? Why don't you try a health farm and let other people cosset you for a change. Or a cruise – would you enjoy a cruise, perhaps?' Dove was about to remind Maisie that she always suggested a health farm or a cruise and each time that she did Dove would say how much she would dislike either when Maisie started talking again.

Maisie was wearing a pink nightdress and dressing gown in the soft, sweet colour of a marshmallow and Dove could see clearly the child that her mother had been. 'I remember coming to England on one of the Union Castle ships – *Pretoria Castle? Pendennis*? The name's gone for the moment but I can still see my parents dressed for dinner, Verena wearing that long string of pearls that she gave to you.

'Pender was only a baby, of course, but Grenfell and I did much as we wanted all day long. The one thing we couldn't get used to were the restraints on us; the ship seemed so *small* and we felt like internees, circumscribed by water.'

'I thought the Union Castle liners were pretty big and, after all, you were hardly travelling steerage.'

'Oh, it seemed extravagantly luxurious to us all right, but we'd never been so confined before. On the farm I wore Grenfell's old trousers, which was thought decidedly odd in those days, and we both had ponies and rode together for miles across the veldt. My father was away fighting and I don't think my mother ever worried about what we did or where we were.'

'Verena was still a bit like that when Lawry and I lived with them, except that I think she was conscious of the fact that we belonged to someone else and she might be held accountable if anything untoward happened to us.'

The gauzy winged moths of Dove's memories were gathering again around the two women in Maisie's room, gliding and settling around them as Dove thought of the years when she and Lawry had lived with their grandparents. He was the preferred, the chosen one, through whom the Woodvine genes would pass on to another generation. Dove had tried so hard to please them but Lawry, capricious in his affections even then, secure in his grandparents' regard, could do no wrong. Dove had watched and grieved, half-understanding when she was still too young for such knowledge, that she would always be second best.

In those days it had been a young Gracie Beckerleg who had consoled Dove: Gracie with the spare, scrawny body and hair permed into curls like unravelled wire wool, who had diverted her into laughter. Gracie was employed to help Verena with the housework but Verena never noticed whether or not it had been done and Gracie was much happier showing Dove how to crimp pasties or allowing her to beat margarine and milk into the family's small ration of butter to make it go further.

It was sometime during the summer when Dove was seven that Gracie Beckerleg had stopped coming to Rejerrah and the children were told that she was no longer needed now that their mother was able to spend more time with them, her war work discharged. Dove, unpersuaded, had found her way alone through the warren of Penalverne's back lanes to the Beckerlegs' shop, where she was met with some show of facetious astonishment at her enterprise and a door was closed swiftly on the crying of a very young baby.

'People don't really change you know, I've learned that much in my life.' Maisie lifted her hands and let them drift down again onto the arms of her chair. Dove was reminded of a pianist preparing to play but of course there was no sound. 'Verena loved us, I'm sure, but she always seemed uninvolved somehow, as if we hardly belonged to her and she was just minding us until someone came along to claim us back.' Maisie's voice was low, the gentle effort of evocation tiring her. Dove half rose to her feet to guide her mother towards the bedroom but sat down again as Maisie went on, 'I've often thought that perhaps I misjudged her because when Grenfell was killed I thought that she would die as well. I think it was having to support Girlie that kept Verena going; that, and you being born so soon afterwards – or so she always told me.'

'And yet Lawry was always her favourite, we both knew that.'

'No, darling, you're wrong: I've just been trying to explain to you that you're confusing her detachment with indifference, and it's not the same thing at all. I do think, though, that she didn't *allow* herself to feel things in the same way after Grenfell and that may be why you think she loved Lawry more than you. He was already fixed in her affection, you see, and you had to be learned from the beginning, but she adored you, Dove: why do you think she made me promise that I would give Rejerrah to you?'

'Why did she, Maisie?'

'Because she knew that you weren't afraid of the responsibility of a house like this. Lawry was so like Matabele Jack that Verena knew what he would do – sell it or break it up into flats or have holiday cottages built in the gardens.'

Dove wondered if Maisie could possibly know of the way in which Lawry had tried to persuade her to capitalise on Rejerrah and to allow him to manage it for her. He had lost his money in a similar scheme already but used every weapon he possessed to convince Dove that he had learned from the experience and that he couldn't fail again. Dove had refused to consider his ideas and there had developed a coolness between them, Lawry moving always further towards the south east of England in a series of jobs in mediocre hotels and golf clubs, where he talked of 'm'people in Cornwall and m'family's place'. He lost his wife, Virginia, somewhere between Bray and Henley-on-Thames but by the time that Lawry married Loretta any animosity towards Dove had long since been dissipated. He needed Dove's acceptance and, erratic as he was, Lawry's saving grace was that he bore no grudges. Unlike Dove, who forgot nothing and forgave little.

Dove would have liked to continue the conversation with Maisie but looking towards her mother she saw that she was almost asleep, dozing lightly with her mouth open and her head fallen sideways like a baby in a pushchair. Dove woke her gently and saw her to bed, leaving to infiltrate once more her own house of esoteric concealment and puzzling over the words which Maisie had said so softly that Dove wondered if she had heard them at all: 'Verena knew the secret, you see.'

After a little nap Maisie often found it hard to go back to

sleep and now she lay awake in her pale yellow bedroom; the primrose curtains were drawn, the pleated ivory silk lampshade softly luminous. Maisie slept rather upright and two plump pillows supported her like a bird in a down-filled nest. Her fingers seemed to have a need of their own to be busy and even now they smoothed and stroked bouquets of wild roses and forget-me-nots scattered in irregular patterns over the quilt on her bed.

Maisie's eyes skimmed the walls painted the previous spring by Jossy in Sudbury Yellow. They had chosen the colour together, Jossy reading earnestly from the paint chart that Sudbury Yellow was an interpretation of the wall colour for the staircase at Sudbury Hall in Derbyshire. Maisie thought it looked like semolina and they had laughed together at the pretentiousness of names but Jossy had reported that the paint was brilliant to use so they had consulted the chart once more and found a colour called Wainscot to use in Pender's bedroom. It was the colour that coats the walls of unreconstructed pubs, only years of assault by nicotine achieving such shade and patination. Pender had refused to allow his room to be decorated, preferring, he claimed, the green tongue and groove boarding which had been there before the alterations which had made a second bedroom out of the bootroom of the main house.

The tiny kitchen Jossy had painted cream and red, stencilling poppies onto the cupboard doors and hiding the plumbing under the china sink with a gingham curtain. Maisie's specially adapted bathroom became what Jossy called a beachscape, painted waves lapping halfway up the walls, spume crested, with a floor the colour of wet sand. She had edged a piece of glass with driftwood onto which she had stuck small shells which she selected with generous deliberation from a boxful she had collected over the years. Large grey pebbles piled on the windowsill and a piece of netting slung across a corner for odds and ends completed her design. Luckily Maisie thought it all very taking, moving aside just a few of the larger stones to make room for her own bathroom necessities. She had given Jossy a free hand to do what she liked to the flat except in the sitting room, and here Maisie had insisted on sage green and a pink the colour of old, crushed bricks.

Now, lying in the cocoon of her bed, Maisie thought of Jossy and how much more she knew about her than Dove did. Dove lingered insistently in Maisie's mind as she fell asleep with the light still on, wondering if she was wrong to have encouraged her daughter to go on holiday. Should she, Maisie wondered, have told her to stay; warned her not to abandon Lewis to Anita Fielding's covert predation. Her last thought was that it was too late now anyway.

Anita Fielding, Cody and Freya moved into the flat above the garage in the middle of the following week. It rained all day, horizontal drizzle alternating with downpours of squally showers, blown every way by the kind of wind which seems to get under your very skin.

They appeared to have little luggage for three people. The children carried multi-coloured rucksacks; their fashionable, kaleidoscopic clothes seeming to provide insufficient barrier to the weather. Anita herself was dressed in an ersatz Puffa, too bright and too fashionable. She was animated and seemed not to mind the rain as she ran up and down the outside staircase to the flat. She had very thin legs and they looked to Dove as wilful and uncontrolled as those of a five-year-old, toes pointing in, knees exposed by too short a skirt, their vulnerability emphasised by the tight black leggings Anita wore tucked into chunky boots, as she unpacked bags and smallish boxes from the back of Pender's car.

Dove watched the activity from the vantage point of

Maisie's kitchen window. Enid Glazzard had called earlier to take Maisie out to lunch and an afternoon of euchre, so Dove was alone in the house. She saw Pender close the boot of his car and open one of the rear doors, struggling to grasp and balance a television set as he slowly mounted the steps, slippery from the rain.

Pender didn't appear again for a long time and Dove imagined him plugging in the wires and tuning in the channels so that the children could watch videos while their mother made coffee for him, fussing around like an animated, puffball-haired doll. Pender had never mastered the intricacies of anything mechanical and Dove knew that he would be unsuccessful in setting up the television. Later on, she suspected, Lewis would be fetched to rectify Pender's ineptitude.

Dove did wonder if she, herself, should make coffee and take it across to the flat as a gesture of acceptance but she hadn't quite forgiven Pender for his manipulation of the situation and she dismissed the idea almost at once. Dove had persuaded Diana to help her to clean the two rooms and bathroom which made up the flat, and they had left a heater on all night to disperse a lingering but not unpleasant smell like a remembrance of the hay and straw which had been stored there, long ago. Dead wasps lay dry and dust-covered in corners of the windowsills, trapped in the autumn before they could escape and Dove swept them into the dustpan, cobwebs clinging stickily to the bristles of her brush.

Lizzie, a friend of Bethan's, had been the last person to stay in the flat and the walls were still marked where pieces of Blutak had fixed posters to every flat surface. They had looked, Dove remembered, as if they had been home-made: 'green', Lizzie had explained as if this were description enough. At the time Dove had thought very irksome the lectures on agri-economy and a barter system that Lizzie was trying to set up among her friends, and had been provoked beyond measure at the continuous, needling homily about the waste of resources that the garden at Rejerrah represented. Once, indeed, Dove had wondered aloud if Blutakking posters to someone else's walls was also considered to be 'green', and had been made to feel petty and grudging in her response to the greater needs of Planet Earth.

In the end Dove had asked Lizzie to leave and in the ensuing discord Bethan had gone too, and had never really lived at home again. Bethan had been reasonable but adamant and Dove had watched her go, knowing that she had handled the situation badly. To all outward appearances things were just the same but Dove knew that her own intransigence had caused irreversible hurt and now Bethan was living with a twice-divorced man only a few years younger than Lewis and for whom Dove had to simulate affection or allow the separation from her daughter to grow wider. It was a penance which Dove fulfilled with bitter proficiency.

After a while Dove grew tired of waiting to see if Pender would appear again down the steps from the flat and she wandered away from the kitchen window into Maisie's sitting room. It was, Dove thought, a pretty room, twice the size of either of the bedrooms and with a good view of anyone coming up the drive to the front of the house. It smelled, as did the whole flat, of drying apples; it was something Dove had often noticed but for which she could think of no explanation.

Dove sat on the wide window seat, on cushions made from pieces of carpet, their faded rose and burnt orange patterns fused into a muted, threadbare elegance. The curtains were the colour of roof tops in Siena, pleasing to the touch, darker than Maisie's velvet-covered chair, and there was a jug of tulips on a low table in the shadows along the far wall. The jug had belonged to Verena and was of silvered pottery, worn through and pale around the rim from years of use, but Maisie was particularly fond of it and it set off the ragged yellow of the tulips, their leaves almost the green of the carpet, both as soft as old jade.

Propped against one of the silver candlesticks on the mantelpiece was the photograph which Maisie had shown Dove of Lawry and his misleading companions. Dove took it down and went back to her seat in the window to look more closely at the other people in the picture. Loretta was certainly there, behind Lawry's shoulder, overlooked when Maisie and Dove had first scrutinised the photograph, withdrawn almost into the background but undoubtedly part of the group. The face, caught by the flashgun, was as smooth and monochrome as a boiled egg, a slight sheen over the high cheekbones and eyes as pale and private as smoky glass. What had Lawry seen in her, Dove wondered, so colourless and so absurd in her outspoken assessment of situations about which she knew next to nothing.

There was, Dove was somewhat surprised to have noticed, every appearance of genuine affection between her brother and his new wife: no unconcealed passion for each other, but the exchange of understanding smiles, the touch in passing of a hand to a head; a certain air, even at this early stage of their marriage, of belonging.

On Sunday Loretta had asked if next week she might go to St John Bosco with Maisie, and Pender was happy to relinquish his rôle of chaperon, anticipating a walk with Sandy to a café on the road to Heamoor where he would eat two bacon sandwiches and drink strong, sweet tea while he read the kind of newspapers of which neither Dove nor Maisie approved. These papers furnished him with nuggets of gossip with which he could divert Girlie and Enid, the scurrility modified by the propriety of Pender's editing.

Dove could find no excuse to linger in Maisie's flat and left by the front door to avoid any possibility of meeting her new tenants. Beyond the dividing wall, in her own part of the house, she drifted from room to room. Very faintly she could hear music from upstairs and knew that at least one of the girls must be at home. Lawry and Loretta, Dove remembered from a conversation at breakfast, were going to visit estate agents that morning and Dove felt herself unsecured, ungrounded, by the lack of demands on her time which the empty house presented.

There was plenty to do: tonight's dinner to prepare; a parcel of books for Bethan which needed to be re-addressed and taken to the post office in town; ironing, always ironing no matter how often she did it. Dove had been surprised by an offer from Loretta to do some laundry for her, and more surprised still by the competent way in which she had accomplished it. 'Goodness,' Dove said, 'Lewis will think it's Christmas, his shirts looking so beautiful.'

Loretta had smiled. 'Oh, I'm good at ironing, and darning too, although no one else seems to darn anything any more. And I can polish properly and remove stains and I actually do dust the legs of the chairs.'

'A treasure, in fact.'

'We all have talents, Dove, and mine may be small and domestic but they shouldn't be disregarded because of that.'

Dove had felt chastened: she wanted to ask Loretta where she had lived before she had met Lawry; what was her job, her background, but each time that she felt she might engage her sister-in-law in a confidence, Loretta had changed the subject, moving adroitly to neutral ground. She was, Dove was beginning to understand, not altogether as ingenuous as she would appear.

Dove did what she always did in moments of indecision and fetched her notebook from the dresser in the kitchen. She looked again at the unrecognised number written on the cover and, almost without thinking about it, she dialled the figures and waited. It rang for a long time, sounding hollow and abandoned, Dove hardly attending, her mind occupied with plans for an elaborate pudding she would make for dinner. Just as she decided to replace the receiver a voice said, 'Hello.'

'Oh,' Dove was disconcerted and said the first thing that came into her head. 'Is Enid there?'

'No one here called Enid.' In the background there was the sound of a child grizzling, accompanied by the bump and tinkling of a toy being misused. 'I've just moved in but there was another woman here, youngish with two children – don't know if she was called Enid though – OK?'

'Yes. Yes, thank you. Sorry for disturbing you.' Dove hooked the handset back onto the wall. It could have been Pender, of course, who had scribbled the number on the cover of Dove's notebook, but she knew that it wasn't. It was Lewis's writing, Dove allowing herself to believe that he had been negotiating for Pender, collaborating with her uncle in the pursuit of Anita Fielding.

Dove decided on a pudding called Sylvabella and as she needed to buy the ingredients it required, she started a list:

1. 6 LARGE *eggs*
   Best dark choc x 8 ozs
   Miniature of rum
   Sponge fingers
2. *Take B's parcel to PO – re-address first*
3. *Book holiday*

She couldn't think of anything else and closed the notebook, obliterating the telephone number with two thick strokes of her pen.

The telephone rang as Dove was shrugging herself into her waterproof jacket. She thought about not answering it but it rang on insistently and she picked it up with one hand, the other still fumbling with the heavy brass zip. It was Luke, and Dove wished that she had left the 'phone to convey to him that the house was empty, that no one was there to offer him any expectation of reconciliation with Diana. Dove promised to pass on a message; enquired after Luke's wellbeing, immediately regretting that she had done so and rather tersely cutting him off while he was still answering her question. She wrote a note for Diana and stuck it on the cork board next to the telephone before tying on a scarf and fetching a shopping bag which could be closed tightly against the rain and into which she put Bethan's parcel.

It took Dove forty minutes to walk into town, to visit the supermarket and to take the package to the post office. It was still only mid-morning and she decided to walk the long way home, taking a side road which led down to the quay. The tide was in and winter-tidy boats floated on air, attached to the harbour wall only by ropes, frilled and trimmed with festoons of seaweed like emerald ribbons. It was, Dove knew, just a trick of the light but the boats seemed suspended, the water pockmarked with rain, and purple in the winter morning. Further off, as far away as she could see, the Mount, too, lay skimming the surface of the water, rising out of a haze which covered the horizon and bleached the sun into dissolving rays of light like a picture Dove remembered from Sunday School of the Holy Ghost descending from the heavens.

The rain had changed to a soft drizzle and she spread a plastic bag on the sea wall where it was low enough for her to sit down overlooking the open-air swimming pool and the rocks from where the more intrepid swam. The promenade stretched in a gentle curve past shops and houses which were flooded regularly by high spring tides, past the big hotel and smaller guest houses, past the pavilion and the tennis courts and the bowling green.

When Lawry and Dove were children there had been two lions *sejant* who squatted, one each side of a flight of shallow steps whose stone sparkled with mica and which led to a raised walk and benches set in sloping granite walls. Each lion had a barley sugar pole, a stationary merry-go-round; paint roughened by salt spray, their sun-warmed flanks were a magical ride. The pavilion was brash and fronted by strip lights now but the little shop was still there where Dove and Lawry had tasted their first ice cream after the war, runny, like unset blancmange, on a square of greaseproof paper. For years, outside the shop, there had been an ice cream in a cone taller than Dove herself and in her mind it still smelled of summer; of vanilla and suntan oil and cardboard.

The memories of growing up together brought Lawry so painfully clearly into Dove's mind that she could almost imagine him sprawled beside her, heels kicking the stones of the wall to make the sand fly out of his sandals. Anyone passing who happened to look at the face of the middle-aged woman sitting in the rain on a plastic bag might wonder about her, perhaps giving her a wide berth, unwilling to be drawn into conversation with someone who smiled so to herself.

The memories that pleased Dove were all from a time when she and Lawry had been young; when they roamed together through Penalverne, sure of a welcome at the houses where they called for diversion in their nomadic progression around the town. Verena considered comics to be a waste of money – one of the few things on which she seemed to have an uncompromising opinion – so Lawry and Dove would go regularly to friends whose toy cupboard had a shelf full of progressively dog-eared copies of *Beano* and *Radio Fun* and *Chick's Own*. Sometimes Dove enticed Lawry into the dim, sharp smell of the cobbler's shop where William John Behenna, fingers tanned as dark a brown as the leather he cut and stitched, told them jokes which Dove never really understood, but which she was warned by Lawry never to repeat in Verena's hearing.

They stood together in the entrance to the forge, well out of the way of the reach of impatient legs; carthorses' heavy with matted feathers, or the oiled and shining hooves on the kind of ponies Dove coveted but of which she was shamefully afraid. The forge always seemed to be full of people watching Billy Beckerleg hammering and tempering the shoes he fitted to horses all day long. Billy Beckerleg was Gracie and Cissie's brother and always had a smile for the Eustace children. 'My little maid an' that 'ansome great boy', he called them, often slipping sixpence into each receptive hand. There were no dubious jokes in the forge, but talk of the Chapel and the war and, once, the wonder of the sky flaming like a winter sunset when Plymouth had burned all night, the docks afire from German bombs.

Dove, two years younger than her brother, had always been the leader, even then sturdy and uncompromising. Lawry allowed himself to be led and Dove never had any hesitation about using the advantages of being the granddaughter of Matabele Jack Woodvine. Now, over forty years later, looking along the promenade Dove could see the faded green lions on which she and Lawry had sat so often when they were small and she remembered when her school sandals, worn thin and crinkled and comfortable, had touched the ground on either side and she had known with a terrible eclipsing anguish that she had grown too old to ride a lion any more.

Matabele Jack had told her that she was now old enough

to take on real lions and that he was going to tell her something very important that he had learned in Matabeleland a long time ago. 'If you ever meet a lion,' he had said, 'what you have to do is stand your ground, look him straight in the eye and when he's near enough, quick as you like, reach into his mouth, catch hold of his tongue and go on pulling until he turns inside out.' Jack Woodvine had leaned back in his chair, stick and cigar emphasising his point. 'Never give you any more trouble after that. Remember that Dove, be useful to you all your life.'

Dove had read that the lions were going to be removed, redundant, stored in a scrap yard with broken fridges and leaky, rusty boilers. Already, the grey pavement of her childhood had been replaced by pink paving slabs: flecks of gold no longer sparkled in the sun as they did from the tall granite houses and steps and walls all around Penalverne: false gold, but real enough to a child. Dove had never entirely believed in it; it had been Lawry who had tried to chip the flakes out of the rock with a kitchen knife he had taken when Gracie Beckerleg's attention had been distracted. He had broken the blade, of course, but Gracie had not betrayed him.

A car passed Dove, window down, music tearing through the air. She looked up, annoyed, at the very young man at the wheel, wanting to make some extravagant gesture of disapproval, but he was gone, far down the promenade with his contaminating noise. Dove stood up; her back was stiff from the awkward angle at which she had been sitting and she took time to fold up her carrier bag and to straighten her jacket before walking slowly back to the house. She tried not to think about Lawry any more because it saddened and confused her that they had grown so far apart. If it wasn't for Loretta, she thought, perhaps things might have worked out even yet, but Dove knew that her sister-in-law was someone who would never naturalise with the family and against whom they must be on their guard. Loretta's apparent inability to separate frankness from responsible reticence was a danger over which Dove knew that she must prevail.

7

Girlie never wore mauve. It was her sister's colour and to wear it would have been to take on her sister's character and everything that implied. Ruby Eustace had been dead for a year, mourned scarcely at all by anyone who had known her. She had been conceived on her parents' wedding night and it was as if the shock and agitation of Dolly Pullyn, married for ten hours to Edgar Eustace, had been imprinted on their daughter's personality from the moment of her inception.

Ruby had been the agent of disquiet in the Eustace family; troubled with her nerves, contentious and progressively more deranged, she spent all day, first in front of the radio and later in front of the television set, knitting. Ruby Eustace knitted scarves and mittens and bedsocks: she knitted tea cosies and cardigans and hats, and everything she knitted was mauve. Not just a Tyrian purple but heliotrope and scabious; lilac and magenta and the amethyst of a bishop's ring. She knitted in thick, thin, shaggy, shiny and unravelled wool, cotton and silk. There wasn't a charity shop in Penalverne or a school or church bazaar which hadn't been the recipient of Ruby's beneficence.

When she died half way through *Home and Away* and a violet cardigan, the matron of Carwarthen had filled two black plastic sacks with the products of Ruby's frenetic industry and these she handed over to Enid Glazzard who had come on Girlie's behalf to collect Ruby's possessions.

Girlie and Enid had laid out in piles determined by shade those objects whose creation marked the last few months of Ruby's life. At first they had been amused but as each heap grew, so did Girlie's distress and Enid, watching her friend, suddenly swept everything back into the bags and disappeared with them. Enid, herself, had taken the sacks to the nearest landfill sight, throwing them as far as she could into the accumulated rubbish of Penalverne, the chance of seeing a dustman dressed in an episcopal Aran or a baby in a bonnet the colour and texture suggestive of a Cadbury's wrapper too daunting to contemplate. They were never mentioned again but by the time the story of Ruby's knitting was relayed to Pender and Maisie it had been defused, reduced to farce.

Today, Enid Glazzard had helped Girlie into a dress of her favourite French blue, loose over the hips so that it wouldn't crease as she had to spend so much time sitting down. Enid had fastened the clip on Girlie's chosen brooch, a woven golden basket of jewelled flowers; sapphire, citrine, a blush pink diamond and emeralds, and then lifted Girlie's hair to snap the catch on a triple string of pearls which matched her earrings. A gold watch as thin as a wafer, two old and heavy rings which hung loosely on her fingers and Girlie was ready.

Enid's own preparations took rather less time. Freed from the necessity of clothes of a purely utilitarian nature and with a little money to spare for the first time in many years, she had grown quite adventurous. Brought up in a family of brothers, Enid Glazzard had never submitted to that ultra femininity which women in her position sometimes affected, but had taken the easier road of collaboration and had worn trousers and padded waistcoats and washed out rugby shirts. When her life had become reduced to little more than a daily financial struggle Enid had given up making even the occasional effort to appear dressed more conventionally and had allowed her hair to become untidy and too long, scraped into an unbecoming hairnet or tied back to flow down her back like the tail on one of her horses.

Life with Girlie Eustace had softened Enid and at first, hurriedly and slightly embarrassed, she would try on a dress while Girlie took her time to decide which one or two of her favourites she would buy. Gradually, under Girlie's gentle guidance, Enid had learned what suited her and now had a selection of shirtwaister dresses in the colours which most people found difficult to wear; yellow and lime green and olive, all complemented by heavy jersey knit jackets. Enid's shoes were elegant but sensible, low heeled patent leather pumps or moccasins for everyday and although she refused to have her hair permed or cut short, she had, with initial misgivings, allowed the young hairdresser whom Girlie recommended, to put in lowlights and then a tint, emphasising the natural colour. It was still almost a young girl's bronze, enhanced by the unusual colours Enid now chose to wear. Over the years that Enid Glazzard had been caring for Girlie Eustace she had become *distinguée*, her inherent assertiveness restrained to a level more suited to the drawing rooms of Penalverne and the excellent hotels in which she and Girlie stayed each spring and autumn.

Now, having helped Girlie to dress and leaving her with a cup of coffee within easy reach, Enid opened her wardrobe and selected a dress of burnt orange, patterned all over with what looked like beige and off-white double helices. Her new winter coat was the colour of good milk chocolate and Enid folded inside the neck a Liberty scarf that Girlie had given her for her birthday. She had no jewellery, all her mother's having been sold long ago to pay vet's bills, but she always wore an old watch, its face so yellow and its glass so crazed that her estimation of time was becoming only approximate.

Enid and Girlie were making an expedition: they were going to the travel agents in Truro through whom they booked their holidays. This would be followed by lunch in an hotel during which they would decide whether to drive straight home or whether they would take the lower road, divert at Helston and drive down to look at the sea in Mullion before returning to Penalverne through Marazion, where they knew there was a teashop that stayed open in the winter. There was no need to decide anything in advance and Enid would drink only sparkling water, making up for her restraint by having an extra sherry or two in the evening.

Enid took Girlie to the lavatory before helping her into the car and securing the seat belt around her. Everything between them was comfortable, any initial self-consciousness at their intimate dependence long forgotten.

When they reached Truro, Enid found the badge signifying disablement in the glove compartment, parked outside Gulliver's and propped the timed permit above the steering wheel. As Enid helped Girlie to her feet, Dove Courtney came out of the travel agents, stopped short as if caught in an act of impropriety but managing to smile and cover her confusion with quick chatter of the purpose of Girlie and Enid's visit to the city.

'Stay and have lunch with us, my dear, we thought the Carvery would be nice; it never seems to disappoint us and I do want to hear all about Lawry and his wife: Maisie's been rather cagey on the subject and we haven't seen Pen for ages.' Girlie turned to Enid. 'When did we last see Pender, Enid?'

'It must have been two weeks ago.'

'Two weeks at least because you'd had a card from your cousin in Melbourne . . .'

'. . . And I showed it to Pender as I thought it might interest him. Must be two and a half weeks then, as that was the day I found the library book we thought we'd lost and that was a week overdue already: I remembered the date because it was my father's birthday.' Enid looked pleased with herself and the two women smiled expectantly at Dove.

'I'd love to, I really would, but I have to get back. I promised to take Maisie to the chiropodist and her appointment's at two.'

Girlie considered Dove, both of them knowing quite well that Maisie had been to the chiropodist two days ago. 'Of course, my dear, can't afford to neglect our feet at our age.' A less generous woman would have pointed out Dove's untruth, leaving her to stumble through an even more transparent excuse but Girlie felt concern for Dove. She considered Dove's position to be unenviable, although there were many less perspicacious than Girlie Eustace who thought that Dove Courtney had everything that she could possibly want in life.

Dove, grateful to Girlie for her tact, heard herself saying something impetuous before she turned away with a lift of her hand, very conscious of the brightly coloured brochures in her open wicker basket, talking too much as a deflection of Enid's unconcealed interest. 'I thought we might have a little do; you know, drinks or something, so that our close friends can meet Loretta. Meet the newest Eustace. Gosh, couldn't say "newest Eustace" after a few of Pen's pink gins, could you? Anyway, I'll let you know the date as soon as poss and now I really must fly.'

Girlie and Enid watched her go, Dove's rather solid legs at their best in thick, dark green woollen tights, oxblood loafers polished, hair escaping from the confinement of her chignon like swarf from a lathe. They watched until Dove turned the corner and then Girlie, moving warily, negotiated the two steps down into Gulliver's. John Swift, proprietor and independent travel agent, liked Girlie Eustace and always dealt with her himself. They concluded negotiations for a New Year break in Torquay's best hotel and Girlie indicated an interest in the same hotel's spring Bridge Week.

Enid found Girlie's cheque book for her, filled it in, leaving Girlie only to sign her name. While she did this, Enid prowled along the racks of brochures intent on finding the one that was tantalising her, half-seen in Dove's basket. Enid passed with a sceptical look the happy families in the Sun and Sand section, rejecting after the shortest glance the Young in Heart, where white-haired pensioners exposed even whiter teeth as they gazed in enduringly game attraction at one another. Disappointed, Enid was about to give up when she saw, behind John Swift's desk, a shelf on which were stacked exactly what she was looking for.

'Well, well,' Enid said quietly to herself and walked far enough round the desk to reach the top copy, fold it in half and wedge it between the handles of her handbag. 'Girlie *will* be interested.' John Swift seemed not to have noticed her manoeuvre. He liked to think that, as someone who helped to arrange other people's fantasies, he took confidentiality as seriously as did any other professional: there were more secrets in his private files than Enid Glazzard would ever have guessed.

He held open the door of the car for Girlie, smiling at Enid as she pulled away into the traffic on her way to the Carvery.

Dove was appalled at what she had done. What on earth had she mentioned a party for? She thought about forgetting that she had ever issued such a rash invitation but knew that Girlie's complicity in her lie meant that she must honour the obligation. She drove home, her mind distracted, swinging into the drive of Rejerrah too fast. Lewis's car was coming towards her and Dove turned the steering wheel sharply to the left, bumping over the old, lichen covered edging tiles and ploughing through cyclamen leaves spread out in a cream and malachite pool under the rhododendron bushes.

Dove said a word that Pender used but from which she had, so far, refrained. When she saw that Anita Fielding was driving Lewis's car Dove said the word again, enunciating it so clearly that the other woman wouldn't need the skill of a lip reader to know what it was.

Dove sat still and watched Anita Fielding pick her way along the tyre tracks to the driver's door of Dove's car. 'I'm terribly sorry, Mrs . . . Dove. I didn't see you but I don't think you've damaged your car. Oh, the poor flowers, what a good job it's only the leaves.' Anita's dandelion head was nodding and bobbing in superfluous agreement with every word.

'Perhaps,' Dove said, 'if you'd been looking where you were going instead of playing with the radio in my husband's car, I shouldn't have destroyed all the buds on my autumn cyclamen. Now, if you'll kindly go wherever it was you were going, I'll get back on the path and see whether there *is* any damage.' Dove pressed the button which closed her window and cut off the sound of Anita's voice, not looking at the frightened young woman, aware only of her tentative pale boots among the plants and her own shameful antagonism and overreaction to something which had occurred quite regularly during the years when her daughters were learning, one by one, to drive.

Dove reversed out of the shrubbery, turned off the engine and went back to reinstate the tiles which had been knocked down. They were the colour of liver but mottled with lichen, a forest of tiny golden trees growing from mounds of mossy green and surrounded by flat scalloped rosettes like jade carvings. They were perfect miniature gardens, overlooked and neglected, and Dove was reluctant to push them back into the damp, dark earth. As she straightened up she caught sight of Pender, half-hidden behind the hedge, one arm straight out in front of him at an unnatural angle. She realised that Sandy must be taking him for a walk.

It wasn't just Sandy though who came around the corner with Pender, but the small boy called Cody. 'Taking these two for a blow on the beach.' Pender seemed pleased at the prospect and as the child looked at Dove she saw his small hand creep into the old man's big one. Cody was dressed in jeans and heavy boots and a zipped jacket quartered in black and mauve. It made him look very pale, his eyes sunk in dark circles under a hat worn back to front. He disturbed Dove and she wanted to ask her uncle why Anita Fielding was driving Lewis's car but said only that it looked like rain so they'd better hurry on their way. As they turned the corner she heard Cody's voice start again, like the chirping of a small bird, words blown back to her but dissipated before she could intercept them.

Dove knew that it was unlikely that anyone but Maisie would be in but, nevertheless, she took the travel agent's brochures out of the car, went into the house and locked them into a drawer of her desk, before putting the car away and going around the side of the house to Maisie's back door.

Maisie was watching a schools programme about reproduction and as Dove approached her, Maisie swivelled her eyes towards her daughter only long enough to say, 'Just *look* at this, Dove: if we'd had programmes like this years ago think of the anxiety we should all have been spared.' Dove looked. A stallion was covering a mare who stood docile and seemingly uninterested, her tail held aside by one of the several men gathered around her.

'If I'd seen that it certainly wouldn't have decreased *my* anxiety, just given me all the wrong expectations.' She laughed and picked up the remote control, switching off the set without asking Maisie if she minded. 'Saw Girlie and Enid in Truro, going into Gulliver's.' Dove watched Maisie's hands pick up her crochet and continue to work a long and complicated chain without hesitation while Maisie looked at Dove, aware that the remark was only a contrivance.

'Booking their next holiday, I suppose.' Maisie said no more, waiting, concentrating on turning a corner.

She didn't have to wait long as Dove said suddenly and much too loudly, 'I've done something really idiotic: can't *imagine* why, but I told them that I was going to have some sort of party to introduce Loretta to people, and now I feel I've got to go through with it.'

'That's not so bad.' Maisie considered for a moment. 'In fact, I think it's quite a good idea; get it over all at once instead of having to explain her, piecemeal, to everyone. When were you thinking of having it? We could do it together instead of our usual Christmas party and then it wouldn't make much work at all.'

'I suppose so. Or a celebration of them moving out – a sort of house cooling.'

'Is it so bad? They seem to have kept out of the way quite a bit and Loretta does help you, doesn't she?'

Dove closed her eyes, seeing Loretta's ash-coloured clothes and her hair that Diana had described as looking like a cowpat, and felt forlorn: her own ungenerous refusal to help her brother pricked her conscience while she tried constantly to justify to herself the decision she had made.

Dove ignored her mother's question. 'As if that wasn't bad enough, I told Girlie a lie as well – *and* she knew it. Said I couldn't have lunch with her and Enid as I had to take you to the chiropodist this afternoon. And then I drove over the cyclamens just inside the gate as Anita

Fielding came tearing down the drive in *Lewis's* car, if you please.'

'Pen did mention that she had to take Freya somewhere – the asthma clinic, I think he said – and, of course, it's very difficult if you don't have a car. So he took Cody – what an extraordinary name, don't you think – out with him and Sandy, and Lewis took Diana's car.'

'Why didn't Anita Fielding take Pen's car?'

'Oh, I don't think he'd lend her the Princess – there are limits even to Pen's generosity.'

'But not to Lewis's, apparently. Good job I managed to swerve into the bushes to avoid her or Lewis and I might both have ended up carless. Why hasn't she got a car of her own, for goodness' sake?'

'I believe she did have, but Pender says her husband took it back when she left him; chased her for miles in a taxi and when she had to stop for petrol, he threw all her things out onto the road and left her stranded in Liskeard with the two children, both terribly upset, of course.'

'I'm not surprised, anyone'd be upset being stranded in Liskeard. What did she do next?'

'As her husband had taken the car, Anita took his taxi back to Penalverne, found a Bed and Breakfast for a couple of nights while she looked around for a house to rent.'

'You mean she was *leaving* Penalverne?'

'Oh, yes. Going to stay with her sister in Wiltshire, I believe, but she decided that, after all, she might be better off if she stayed here.'

'As she so obviously is, with a choice of cars and a besotted old man as baby-sitter and universal provider.'

Maisie looked at her daughter, Dove's face maliciously amused, and wondered what to say. Was now the right time to warn Dove? Would it ever be the right time, or should Maisie keep her own counsel, listening to Pender who said that he would continue to draw the fire of public derision in the hope that Lewis's infatuation would prove to be just that, and that Dove need never know the extent of her husband's perfidy.

'And now they've ended up here?' Dove was cautious, remembering the impatient voice on the telephone when she had dialled the unrecognised number on her notebook. Something occurred to her and she spoke more firmly. 'You seem to know an awful lot about her, Maisie: I thought you'd be on my side after seeing how Pender conned me into allowing them to use the flat.'

'I don't understand the ins and outs of it all,' Maisie avoided Dove's eye, 'but Pender somehow got caught up in it. He said he felt terribly sorry for her with those two children and nowhere to live. I suppose,' Maisie said, 'we can't understand what it must be like, but dear old Pen's been on his uppers a time or two and he's been a pushover for a pretty woman all his life, you know that.'

'But it's *my* house, Maisie, not Pen's. And anyway, I don't understand how this woman can be homeless. I seem to remember there was a husband so surely he has to provide for her?'

'In the long run I suppose he will have to.' Maisie hesitated, glancing at Dove's disapproving expression; her daughter looked grudging, Maisie unwilling to formulate the word *hard* in relation to Dove. 'But, you see, *she* left *him*: took the children and fled, so to speak.'

'Without having anywhere to go?'

Maisie said patiently, 'I told you that she was going to her sister but her husband caught up with her and she didn't know what to do so came back to Penalverne.'

'Where Pender just happened to meet her and offered her a home.'

'Dove, darling, do try to understand. Little Mrs Fielding was running away from a husband who beat her up. Taking her children to safety.'

There was a silence, then Dove said, 'Do you believe that, Maisie?'

'I do, because Pen's seen the bruises. Well-hidden, he says, in places covered by her clothes under normal circumstances, but they're there all right.'

'Where's the husband now?'

'Disappeared, I believe, and because their house was rented and the six months was up Anita really was stranded.'

'What will she do for money?'

'No idea. I suppose there are the Social Services.' Maisie was vague, the idea of having no money at all incomprehensible to her.

'She'll have to work.'

'She *had* a job at the Yacht Club but Freya's asthma started to get worse – hardly surprising really given the atmosphere there must have been – and the Committee didn't want someone who had to take so much time off, so they sacked her.'

'And that's where she was going today, to the asthma clinic with the child?'

'Yes, and there's another thing, Dove: if Anita and the children weren't in the flat, then you could hardly have refused to allow Lawry to use it could you, and which would you prefer, after all?'

'You think I should allow Lawry and that frightful Loretta to stay at Rejerrah, don't you?'

'He *is* my son, darling, and I can't take sides, but he's beginning to look so *defeated* that it makes me sad.' Maisie's face looked crumpled and old but Dove ignored it and Maisie went on, 'When your children are unhappy, you feel so responsible. Even at Lawry's age I want to tell the people he worked for and who rejected him that he just needs another chance; to make other people see the good in him that I have never doubted is there.' Maisie allowed her crochet to fall into her lap, fingers still entwined in thin beige cotton which would be turned into swans and snowflakes and flowers by her skill.

'If they stay here you know that we'll all be caught up in his next failure and I'm just too tired to want to go through all that again. I know that he's tried to borrow money from Pen and I suspect that you've lent him some, but don't you honestly think that it's time Lawry learned that he has to earn what he spends?'

'*You* never had to learn that did you?' Maisie's words were soft, disappearing silently into the atmosphere like raindrops on a dusty road. 'Be fair, Dove, you've never had to work like Lawry has; you've never had to *prove* that you could do it.'

Dove looked at her mother. The old woman's eyes were beseeching and Dove felt years of resentment clawing at her, threatening to tear away the precarious restraint with which she had always managed to protect herself. She felt her throat tighten and start to ache as she struggled to control threatening tears. 'What chance have I ever had to prove that I could do anything? All I've ever done is to look after this house and to work in the garden, almost singlehanded, for years: I've cooked and cleaned and been nurse, chauffeur, accountant. I was always the one to get up in the night; the one to discipline the girls so that Lewis was seen as the soft touch; and Lawry always came to *me* when things went wrong for him.

'I organised Lewis's life so that all the boring bits were taken care of; bills paid, visits to the dentist arranged; his car was always taxed and serviced and he just took mine if he needed it, never mind how inconvenient it might have been for me.' Dove stopped, unaware that tears were coursing down her face, dripping onto her clean, ironed jeans.

'It was your choice to stay at home, Dove, no one made that decision for you.' Maisie felt a tightening in her chest and automatically put out her hand for the small brown bottle of tablets which always stood within reach. She put one under her tongue and went on, speaking gently. 'It's different now that the girls are independent and you've got time on your hands, I do understand that – but I think that's a different problem altogether.'

It was as if Dove hadn't heard her mother's voice. 'It's not just at home, either. I've stood for *years* in church halls and on windy corners, serving teas and collecting money or sorting through dirty old jumble. I've taken smelly old men to their hospital appointments – and had to disinfect the car afterwards. I've chased people to buy raffle tickets and donate prizes – and don't think I've never known how they tried to avoid me – and I've potted up *hundreds* of plants for sale and baked literally *dozens* of cakes myself to make money for good causes, and all the time I've been looking after the girls; always interested in whatever they were doing, encouraging them to use their natural talents; putting up with their moods and horrible friends and their food fads.' Dove seemed unable to stop.

'And now your wandering boy only has to come home and plead poverty once again and it's, "Oh, Dove will turn up trumps. Good old Dove, she always does." I'll tell you something, Maisie, the parable I really *do* understand is the one about the Prodigal Son: welcome back to the one person who's never given anything to anyone and ignore the other who's spent a lifetime trying to please everybody.'

'Oh, Dove! Dove, no, it's not like that at all.' Maisie half rose from her chair in agitation but sank back as if her legs were too weak to hold even her small weight. '*Everyone* thinks you're splendid; dependable and responsible and so capable. And what would have happened to me if you hadn't looked after me? I'd probably have ended up knitting in Carwarthen like poor old Ruby. Oh Dove, darling, you've kept the family together for years and we all rely on you totally. You're so strong and so . . .' Maisie tried to find the word which would convey to Dove the strength of their dependence, '. . . so *unfailing.*'

Dove was watching the damp patches on her jeans spread outwards; salty circles of tears touching each other, joining and creeping together. She didn't understand why her trousers were damp until Maisie stood up again, pulled a man's handkerchief from her sleeve and started to dry Dove's eyes as if she were a child, the old, brown-spotted hand gently cradling her daughter's chin. Dove's voice was raw, 'It's not just Lawry, of course, I think I could cope with him on his own. It's Loretta, Maisie. I can see that everyone else is beginning to like her, or at least to not dislike her, and I can't stand her. I'm afraid all the time of what she'll say and I just don't want her around.'

Maisie put the handkerchief into Dove's hand, wrapping her fingers around it as if she were still a little girl. 'Blow your nose, Dove, while I find us both a drink, and then I'm going to tell you something about Loretta which may help.'

Maisie came back into the room with two glasses of sherry. 'I remember now that Pen said he was going to the off-licence today and this is all I could find. It's Enid's special and not too bad really; anyway, it'll buck us up. God Bless!' Maisie lifted her glass towards Dove in a sketchy toast and Dove drank eagerly as if she were thirsty, the anodyne liquid scorching her aching throat.

The room was very quiet; the early winter evening colonising the corners with its advance troops of dusk and shadow, the light outside a deepening blue but here, in this still room, already an illusion of the night to come. Dove felt detached; loss of composure and sherry in the afternoon, almost unprecedented experiences in her life, combining to soothe her emotions. She hovered in a state of drowsy tranquillity where nothing seemed quite real, until eventually Dove felt herself sliding gently into oblivion.

Maisie watched her daughter, plain and uncompromising

in sleep, and wondered why she hadn't told Dove that she loved her. 'Steadfast' and 'reliable' were words that many a committee chairman had used of Dove Courtney but how many people, Maisie wondered, had told her lately that she was loved. Lewis? Perhaps. Diana? Bethan? Unlikely, but Jossy might have done so. Pender was always telling Dove that he loved her but his words were devalued by his insistence that so, too, did Sandy, although Dove never wavered in her antipathy towards the animal that Pender always referred to as his foster-dog.

As Dove slept, Maisie thought of her own parents as she did so often these days: of Matabele Jack Woodvine, a rogue, an adventurer and ultimately, like most of the men she had known, an unfaithful husband. She thought of Verena, drifting self-possessed and untroubled through a life of privilege until that life became almost meaningless with the unforeseen death of her elder son. Matabele Jack's death nine years after Grenfell was something which seemed hardly to register with Verena: the silence in the house; the absence of smoke from her husband's pipe; her solitary state allowing her to sit and read or to write letters without being interrupted, was seen by her as a positive benefit, as it was to be able to sleep, alone and undisturbed, in old linen sheets, worn soft and comfortable from years of vigorous laundering.

Maisie, widowed herself in the last full year of the war, was living with Lawry and Dove in her parents' home when Matabele Jack had died in 1949 and the small household of two women and two children continued very much as before, augmented now and again by Pender, who seemed so often to be between jobs. Maisie walked out occasionally with an admirer but no man ever came even close to disrupting the life of the women at Rejerrah.

When Dove had married Lewis Courtney, he had understood from the first that he wouldn't be expected to find a separate home in which to start married life but was expected to live at Rejerrah and that Dove's mother and grandmother were part of the contract he was undertaking. Lewis, with no close ties of his own to speak of, welcomed the idea and, for some years at least, he mistakenly considered himself to be the head of the family. When Verena died, Maisie assumed her mother's place and Dove, in her turn, moved into her rôle as heiress apparent.

It was Pender who was the catalyst which brought about the conversion of the back of Rejerrah into a separate unit. He finally gave up pretending to work, deciding that without the inconvenience of having to find money for rent, he could manage reasonably well on his pension and a very small income from those investments which he had managed to overlook and which were, therefore, still intact. Pender with his, almost, unconscious charm and his ruthlessness, anticipated no difficulty in persuading Dove to allow him to live at Rejerrah but to his genuine surprise Dove had said no.

Dove qualified her refusal with an entirely plausible explanation that with three daughters growing up and with Maisie as well as herself and Lewis already living there, the house was full and she wasn't prepared to take out of permanent commission the remaining guest bedrooms. And, no, the flat over the garage was in use all the time by the girls and their friends.

Lewis felt sympathetic towards the older man, seeing him as a potential ally in his household of women and had suggested to Dove that they might easily turn the small rooms at the back of the house into a flat where Maisie and Pender could live together. Lewis's expectation of the benefit to him of a supportive male presence was short lived. Pender's friendships were almost entirely with women, some of whom produced in him the kind of adolescent passion which Dove, in particular, found vexing and absurd.

She could accept his lifelong devotion to Girlie Eustace, she understood that; but she found it difficult not to allow her distaste to become obvious as Bunty and Phyll, Monica and Daphy wended their fragrant and well-shod way through her uncle's affections and the gardens at Rejerrah, the privacy of which she guarded so solicitously and through which her uncle paraded his chosen companions, allowing them to admire what they pretended to believe was his domain.

When Dove woke, Maisie seemed to have forgotten that she had promised to tell her something about Loretta and was watching *Fifteen to One* very quietly, not wanting to waken the sleeping woman. Dove looked at her mother for a while through half-open eyes, aware that she had slept in an awkward position and that now she had a bad headache and a dry, fuzzy mouth. For a moment, just before Dove became fully awake, she had thought that it was Verena sitting in Maisie's chair and she was afraid, seeing her mother so suddenly as an old woman.

'Feeling better?'

'Bit of a head but, yes, better than I did.'

The compère of the show was signing off. *'And in answer to your question, Mrs Oxenford of Tunbridge Wells, the G stands for Gladstone.'*

'I'm sorry, Maisie, I shouldn't have said all those things: I didn't even mean half of them.'

'You're overstretched, my lovey; you do too much for all of us and it's bound to come out sometime. What about that holiday you said you'd look into?'

'I picked up some brochures today.' Dove hesitated, then smiled and said, 'I'll tell you when I've definitely made up my mind.' She winced as she pushed herself out of the chair. 'Better go and take some jollop for this headache and have a shower. Can't have anyone seeing me like this.' And Dove

Courtney, wife, mother and thoroughly good woman, let herself out of her mother's back door and went into her own part of the house to put a shoulder of lamb into the oven and to start a list of guests for her party, unaware that her husband longed only for her to show more interest in him and that her daughters longed for her to show less.

8

'You *can't* ask Luke.' Diana was leaning over the kitchen table, toast in hand, examining Dove's guest list for the party.

'Of course I shall ask Luke, and do keep your greasy hands off my notebook, Diana.' It was too late and Dove watched as a blob of butter dripped onto the open page, glossing and making transparent the paper where it fell. Diana brushed at it with the edge of her hand, spreading the damage further. Dove pulled the book away, replacing it with a plate which Diana ignored, moving towards the kettle which she plugged in, toast still in one hand.

'He won't come.'

'Then you've no need to worry about seeing him.' Dove remembered how short she had been with her son-in-law on the telephone but was determined to effect a reconciliation between him and Diana if she possibly could.

'Are Bethan and that dreadful old man managing to drag themselves away from their compost heaps long enough to put in an appearance?'

'Julius. And he's not dreadful, just . . . a bit different. Yes, they're coming.'

'And who's this Dick O'Brian? He sounds like a racehorse trainer.'

'You're on the right track.' Dove was amused, Diana's

instant, impulsive judgement of people often accurate beyond her own careful appraisal. 'He's actually a semi-retired priest, a friend of Pen's. They study form together but your uncle is the only one who will venture into that den of iniquity in Causewayhead where they place their modest bets.'

'Typical!' Diana had found an old jar of Horlicks and was chipping away at the inch thick crust which had formed on top of the powder. She was unsuccessful and left the bottle and lid scattered separately, the bowl of the spoon she had been using bent at an unnatural angle to the handle. She had an unfailing ability to leave Dove's kitchen utensils looking as if they had been trial runs for Uri Geller. The drinking chocolate proved more accessible and Diana settled at the table with her mug and a banana. 'The girls are coming, of course, but what about the glamorous Anita? Or Sylvie Beckerleg, for that matter?'

'Why on earth should I ask Sylvie Beckerleg?'

'Oh come on, Mum, we all *know* she's related to us, and I thought this party was to introduce Loretta to the family.'

'It's for our friends, and Sylvie Beckerleg is not a friend and *certainly* not a member of this family.'

'I can remember her looking after us when Bethan and I were small. She seemed to be a friend then and we didn't like the girl who came after her half as much. She used to make us drink the trifle sherry so we'd go to sleep and she could meet her boyfriend when you were out in the afternoon.'

'That's not true, Diana!' Dove was becoming irritated by her daughter and was feeling guilty that she was irritated. 'I'd have known – and I wasn't out that often.'

'You didn't, and you were.' Diana's voice had lost its edge of amusement and sounded cold and deliberate. 'A committee meeting, any action group, the church, the hospital, you went to all of them. You were always doing good somewhere else and – what was she called again, that girl who came after Sylvie?'

'Kerenza Hockin.'

'And Kerenza Hockin was left to look after us.'

'I don't remember it like that at all. I've spent my life being at home, looking after all of you, never putting myself first.' Dove was looking at Diana in panic, her hands working independently, wiping up the toast crumbs, reuniting the Horlicks jar with its lid, straightening the spoon Diana had used. 'And Kerenza was only here for about six months, after that I didn't have anyone else as you and Bethan were at school all day. Just Mrs Yeoman to help with the cleaning.'

'In the holidays. She was here in the holidays.' Diana sounded triumphant.

'But don't you remember? That was the summer your great-grandmother died and there was so much to do, to sort out, what with Jossy still a small baby, I just had to have some help.' Dove's panic was receding as her memory of those days, nearly twenty years ago, took over. 'The times I had to leave you with Kerenza – and you're quite right, I remember I *was* out a lot that summer – were because Maisie and I were dealing with Verena's estate. It was quite complicated and apart from the business side of it, you've no *idea* how much rubbish she had accumulated.' Dove felt the kettle. It was still warm and she spooned instant coffee into a mug and took her drink to the table, sitting opposite Diana, the notebook between them.

'She had one room *filled* with newspapers, hundreds and hundreds of them stacked in great piles around the walls and they all had to be shifted. I can't tell you how many trips we made to the tip with that lot. And one of the cupboards in her bedroom was *full* of tinned food, lots of it from before the war if you can believe such a thing. We were afraid we'd get ptomaine poisoning if we ate any of it so we threw it all out.' Dove's face was amused. 'And bars of soap.' She looked at Diana. 'Do you know how many bars of soap we found? Guess.'

Diana said tentatively, 'Thirty?'

'Over two hundred! And those were only the used bits: I think she'd been pinching them from the public loo on the prom, poor old bat. Apart from the useless bits, there were dozens and dozens of unopened packets: I didn't have to buy any soap for ages but I was absolutely sick of the smell of Lifebuoy by the time we finished them. She was such a hoarder that she'd kept every paper bag and bit of string and empty box that had come her way for *years* and I remember that one drawer of the little desk on the landing was full of the sticky white paper you get along the edge of stamps. She must have used it before Sellotape was invented and just went on saving it: and there were rubbers, too old and much too hard to use, and inch-long stubs of pencils.'

'I remember some of it, like the sealing wax in the drawer, because the bars were glittery gold and Bethan and I pinched some and hid them in the garden pretending they were buried treasure. And I can remember Great-Grandfather Jack's uniform and Great-Granny's lovely shoes – satin and soft, soft leather and so *tiny*, with sparkly buckles and pretty little heels.' Diana had relaxed, prettier now that her face was less peevish. She looked at her mother. 'What happened to all Verena's things?'

'We threw most of them away.'

'Oh, Mum!'

'I know, I know. I feel awful about it now but back then it was seen as just rubbish – clothes so old nobody could possibly want them. Actually,' Dove hesitated, relinquishing a secret, 'I did keep a few of her things. There was a beautiful cloak, black velvet lined with faded, pink silk, and a couple of dresses that I thought I might use in the evening. Of course, I never did wear them – they're probably still upstairs somewhere if you're interested.'

'If we were all living here together, where on earth did Great-Granny keep all this stuff?'

'Well, her bedroom was where your father and I sleep now and we converted her dressing room into our bathroom, and the guest room on the far side of that was empty so she had three rooms of her own and she crammed them absolutely full with boxes and trunks and brown paper parcels. I'm surprised you don't remember all this, especially those acres of newspapers.'

'I do a bit, but I was always rather scared of Great-Granny. She used to get awfully cross with us and sometimes she didn't seem to know who we were, so we didn't hang around her much; not like we do with Maisie.'

Dove, who remembered Verena as vague and gently detached, thought about this. 'It was losing Grenfell, her elder son, that made her like that, you know. As she got older, she seemed to retreat more and more into a time when Grenfell was still alive. It was more real to her than anything else and I'm afraid little girls were a distraction from the world she was trying to create for herself. It was difficult for all of us, trying to keep things as normal as possible.'

Dove drank her coffee, hardly noticing that it was lukewarm. She was remembering her own mother's tears as Maisie had unpacked a cabin trunk full of Grenfell's toys and school reports. There was an envelope holding a silky curl of pale yellow hair tied with a blue ribbon; his collection of birds' eggs, the medals he had won for running, even his Swan fountain pen and his spectacles, returned to Cornwall at the same time as his clothes and shoes. The shoes were still wrapped in the black tissue paper in which they had been enclosed when they had been brought from London; evidence of repair on the heels but still in good condition, polished, narrower than seemed possible. Maisie had repacked the trunk exactly and for the last fifty years it had stood undisturbed in one of the box rooms in the attic.

It was as if Grenfell's death had directed the family into a pattern from which they had never tried to escape: a shaken kaleidoscope, the pieces settling, always different but always essentially the same. Matabele Jack and Verena had died at their appointed time, both old, both prepared, and Eddie Eustace's death had been so little remarked that it was as if the impression he had made on the family at Rejerrah was no more than a ripple like one of those which marked the place where his ship lay broken into pieces on the sea bed.

If Grenfell had lived, if he had owned Rejerrah and had filled it with a family of his own, all their lives would have been different, Dove knew that. Three generations of women had looked after the house but there was no one person to take it on after Dove. It would have to be sold unless the girls agreed to share it, and Dove thought that unlikely.

'Mum.' Dove was lost long ago in thought and Diana said again, more loudly, 'Mum-*my*.'

'Sorry, I was miles away.'

'No, *I'm* sorry. About saying you weren't there for us. I can see that I got things wrong, the way I usually do.'

'Well, we all muddle things up – your father calls it a selective memory. But I'm glad that now you understand better, it upset me to think you should feel I'd neglected you. I *have* tried you know, Di, to do the best I can for everyone.' Dove wondered if her eldest daughter understood what she was trying to say. 'Just lately though it all seems . . . oh, I don't know, not *enough* somehow. As if I've got everything wrong.' Dove felt again the panic that had threatened her, like something trapped in a part of her that she didn't recognise, lodged where she thought her soul might be.

'No,' Dove put out a hand. 'Don't say anything. You will just say what I would tell a friend who came to me in trouble and it won't help.' She looked at her daughter. 'I shouldn't have said anything to you; it's not your problem and I'll work it out in the end but, please darling, don't talk about it to anyone else, especially not to your father, as he really wouldn't understand.' Dove took a last mouthful of the now cold coffee, grimacing at the bitterness, and pulled her notebook towards her. She smiled faintly at Diana. 'Back to my lists – those I *can* control. What do you think about asking some younger people, friends of Jossy's, perhaps? And then we must start planning the food.'

Diana would have liked to prolong the moment of unusual closeness with her mother but she could see that Dove had made up her mind to concentrate on the trivial, consigning the past to that region where it lived a subdued and largely unexplored life of suppressed memories and unfulfilled resolution. Diana decided that she would go and talk to Maisie later on: her grandmother was always so cheerful and indiscreet and Diana wanted to know the truth about the things that Jossy had only hinted at to her about Anita Fielding and their father.

When Diana had left the kitchen, her hands full of biscuits taken from a packet left torn and open on the shelf, Dove sighed and stood up. She emptied the biscuits into the airtight tin where they should have been stored and swept the crumbs into the palm of her hand. She stood looking at them, little irregular lumps of fat and flour, shiny with crystals of sugar, globules of chocolate melting on her skin even as she watched.

Suddenly Dove felt overwhelmed, as if those small amorphous particles were rocks and boulders, too heavy for her to sustain without injury: disintegrating and fragmenting in her hand; bruising and crushing her flesh, causing it to decay and crumple and fracture. Dove knew that if she allowed the weight of the crumbs to tear her hand apart, then cracks and fissures would spread up her arms, snaking and sneaking across her body, splintering her legs until she shattered into a thousand shards, clinking and dribbling into a cumbersome heap on the kitchen floor. Would anyone sweep up the scraps that had been Dove Courtney? Would they step over her, pushing the detritus aside with a careless foot? Would anyone at all really care that she had been reduced to the inconvenient remnants of a woman who had tried her best but who knew, beyond consolation, that it was not enough?

Dove was still staring at the crumbs in her hand when the kitchen door opened and Loretta insinuated herself into the room. She stood without speaking and looked at Dove and Dove, becoming aware that she was no longer alone, turned her head towards her sister-in-law, raising her hand towards her as if it were hurt – burned or bleeding or grazed. Loretta moved towards Dove, taking the crumb spattered hand gently in her own, running it under cold water from the tap while she spoke quiet, inconsequential words which seemed to come from her mouth rehearsed and known by heart. Loretta reached for the towel which hung on a hook by the sink, patted Dove's hand dry and moved her towards the room beyond the kitchen. Dove allowed herself to be led to a comfortable chair, Loretta sitting next to her on a footstool while she stroked Dove's hand and murmured tenderly as if Dove were a sick child.

Quite suddenly Dove became aware of her position, withdrawing her hands from Loretta's, folding them together to avoid further contact with this unwelcome intruder. Loretta accepted the rejection, silent and watchful as she had learned to be, but no longer afraid of her determined and capable sister-in-law whom she now perceived to be as defenceless as Loretta herself had been when Lawry Eustace had met her on the holiday she had won in a phone-in.

Loretta had been reluctant to go on holiday abroad on her own, being used to the minibus full of old people and a week out of high season spent chaperoning an elderly crocodile protected like children against any reluctant sun in straw hats made gay with scarves and scraps of material tied around the crowns. She was used to never eating a meal uninterrupted by a request to 'go', and to intervening in the quarrels which erupted over nothing – the size of an ice cream, the wrong seat in the coach, the favouritism shown by a second helping of pudding.

Loretta had gradually become invisible; a wiper and a dryer, a tucker-in and a zipper, a listener and a watcher. It suited her: she liked the anonymity, the routine; the sameness of mince on Wednesdays and fish on Fridays, of peppermints and Fisherman's Friends, the best necklace and cardigan when a visitor was expected and the childish excitement of blowing out candles on a cake. It was because Loretta listened to the old women in her care that she had won the phone-in on questions about music hall artistes and because she had listened to her fortune being told in tea leaves that she had applied for a passport, gone to France and met Lawry Eustace on the first night of the holiday.

Old, beautiful Rejerrah was a long way from the unit where Loretta Lyons had spent several years before being returned cured, she was assured, into a world which, at first, she found difficult to comprehend. Her job at Hawthorn Lodge had been a temporary expedient which she grew to enjoy, the routine of the old incarcerated within its bright, malodorous walls not so different from that which Loretta had already experienced for herself, and she liked the women she looked after, who called her darling and said she was a good girl.

Loretta knew that she was not but she had learned better than to tell anyone that she had stabbed her father; stuck him almost to death with the carving knife one Sunday lunchtime when the piece of pork on the table reminded her too powerfully of what she knew would follow the meal when her mother, prayer book in hand, had left the house to collect her sister and then to go on to Benediction together as was their unbreakable habit. Mrs Lyons had missed Benediction that week: Mr Lyons didn't die and Loretta had been driven from the house in a police car, sitting quietly in her blood-stained clothes until she had been taken from the police station to a secure hospital unit.

Loretta's somewhat unconventional responses had confused those assigned to her welfare. She had settled down in the unit, making assessment difficult as she showed no real desire to leave, becoming almost as useful as a member of the staff. It was only the intenseness of her observation of others and a certain lack of reserve which made her conversation more forthright than was considered altogether desirable, that perpetrated the diagnosis that she was not yet ready to find a place for herself outside the unit.

It was the cutbacks in local authority spending that accelerated Loretta Lyons' recovery. When there was no longer any money to pay for her support, she was judged to be cured and sent home to her mother. Mrs Lyons and her sister, whom she had invited to live with her after Mr Lyons had taken himself off, now went to Benediction three times a week and to Mass every morning, and she was not welcoming to the daughter whom she regarded as queer.

Loretta was found a job at Hawthorn Lodge and adjusted to life there just as she had to living in the unit. Her marriage to Lawry Eustace was a progression undertaken with the same unquestioning acceptance with which she had embarked on every stage of her life.

Lawry loved Loretta for her innocence and truthfulness and because she was more vulnerable than he was. Lawry Eustace had never before been *needed* and it was a chance of which he intended to take every advantage, just as he was determined to make Loretta happy.

When Loretta had come so quietly upon Dove in the kitchen she knew from long experience what to do but Dove was discomfited and embarrassed to be seen in even so rare a moment of weakness. Now, she became aware of their relative positions and she withdrew at once from Loretta's concern, looking at the dowdy little figure with unremitting dislike. 'Did you want something, Loretta?'

'I was going to make a cup of tea for Lawry. Would you like one, Dove?'

'No. No, thank you. I've got lots to do, this party I'm organising, but I think I'll just get a breath of fresh air first.' Dove stood up and went into the kitchen passage. She could see Loretta still sitting on the footstool, her skirt, which was both too long and too short, the colour of loganberries mixed with cream, spread around her. She was watching Dove through the open door but neither woman spoke and Dove buttoned her coat and went into the garden.

Dove took an outer path, flagged and slippery at this time of the year, and soon she was lost in concealing greenery. On her left was a wall from which trailed ivy, now heavy with berries, and hart's tongue ferns, toadflax and the bronze-red cushions of little robin which would be covered in pink flowers in late spring. Dove allowed these wild gardens to grow but had planted pittosporum and myrtle trees and these grew legitimately in the warmth and shelter of the wall. On the right-hand side of the path there was a long bed of wild scarlet fuschia, one of the few bright colours allowed to grow at Rejerrah. Dove loved it and indulged its untrammelled progress, but she noticed now that it threatened to overwhelm the snowberry bushes in their effort to claim a share of the light and wondered if it would be wise to move them before they started to shoot again in the spring. She would put it on her list of garden things to be thought about.

The walk ended in shade under the canopy of two copper beeches, where there was a little splashing spring, water jetting down the wall from a moss-lined chute and trickling over rocks, furred and lichened like animals humping their backs in sleep. The effect was of something changeless, although change was of its essence: water droplets like diamonds caught in the fronds of the edging ferns before they dripped into the water causing ripples and eddies to wash against the stones. Twigs and leaves changed the pattern of the water, and the activity of insects: occasionally, even the blue of a dragonfly as it hovered, iridescent, over the tiny pool.

Some people found oppressive this moss-green, shadowy oasis but ever since she was a child, Dove had loved it. No matter how hot and dry the rest of the garden, it was always cool here, the trickle of water constant, seeming to be unaffected by drought or storm. It was the sound of the water, low enough to demand concentration, loud enough to invite enjoyment, that had captured her attention as a small girl and it was here that she had seen fairies dancing in the moonlight, silver shoes brushing the top of the moss without leaving any footprints, glittering water visible through their gauzy wings. Their dresses had been rose and apricot and gold like the big girls at school were wearing for the end-of-term play and which Dove longed with all her heart to be allowed to wear as well. On the fairies' long, wavy hair were coronets of tiny pearls and filigree like the wire inside the electric cable that lay uncoiled in the garage where her Uncle Pender had been attempting, ineffectual as always, to fix up a light.

Dove had told no one what she had seen in the moonlight on that hot June night and for the rest of her life she had never altogether disbelieved it. Now, as her sensible Ecco shoes stood where silver slippers had once skipped and tiptoed in her imagination, Dove Courtney knew that there were no fairies here any more. They had melted away in the light of day, dissolved by the rainbow-bearing water that splashed relentlessly on, the source of which Dove and Lawry had never been able to trace beyond the brook at the edge of the Mennaye Fields as it flowed headlong from Newlyn. She thought, just for a moment, that Loretta might understand, but quickly pushed the thought away, unwilling to allow even a crack to appear in her resistance to Lawry's wife. Loretta's comforting of Dove was something which Dove would not easily forgive, but as she turned the corner, away from the spring and into the main garden, she understood, on a tacit level, why it was that people liked Loretta.

Dove settled on the bench under the Robinia tree. It was too cold to sit outside for long without discomfort but she turned up her collar and pushed her hands into the pockets of her coat, determined to stay as long as she needed to think things through in her own mind. Dove was aware now that what she found disturbing were not those things on the surface of her life: Diana's defection from Luke and the disorder it had caused at Rejerrah, nor the presence of Lawry and Loretta. Her brother and his wife, to her surprise, had caused little disruption and Dove despised herself for fabricating evidence to keep alive her antagonism towards them.

What really troubled Dove was the knowledge, which she could no longer deny, that the transient disaffection she felt for Lewis had become mutual. Lewis was so easy-going, too emotional, too dependent on Dove's moods for her to take him seriously for much of the time and once they had been married for a little while it had aggravated Dove to realise that her husband's reliance on her was not just a newly married man's eagerness to please but that it was the pattern into which their life together was falling.

Dove had accepted this turn of events, making a virtue of necessity, filling her life with other people's needs. Maisie and Pender had taken the girls' place as her daughters, one by one, moved away. She had devoted herself to Rejerrah and to Lewis, to his comfort, his every desire; steeling herself to his approaches when she no longer felt the need for sexual encounter herself. Had he known that? Dove thought not. Lewis had always seemed content with his choir and his rugby and in the summer he walked a good deal and sailed a little. She had thought him contented but lately there had been something different, some defiance of her, that she found perturbing.

Dove had watched her brother and his new wife and there could be no doubt at all that they loved one another. She had watched Pender with Anita Fielding and . . . suddenly, as she sat in her garden surrounding her house and thought about her husband, Dove saw something else. She saw Lewis's face turn away as she described Anita Fielding as 'that dreadful little woman': she saw Cody and Freya running, unafraid, towards Lewis as to a well-known friend, and she saw Lewis silhouetted in the garage doorway looking up at the little flat where laughter was mingled with noise from the television, and all at once Dove Courtney understood without any uncertainty at all the reason for the unfamiliar panic which had become her daily companion.

Dove sat under the Robinia tree which Matabele Jack had planted until she felt too cold to move, her new knowledge a nebulous, frozen centre which she was striving to enclose in practical understanding to diminish its effect; to mitigate the monstrous notion that her husband, to whom she had subjugated her need for a life of her own, was in love with someone else. A woman who wore vulgar clothes and who gave her children affected, prejudicial names; a woman whose hair was bleached and whose eyelashes were dyed; a woman, moreover, without a home or even a car of her own who was living on Dove's charity only yards from Dove herself.

To say that Dove felt mostly indignation is to devalue the depth of her response in the light of such perception, but as she sat uncomfortably on the weathered wooden bars of the bench, unwilling to move because she knew the effort would make her aware once more of the stiffness in her back, Dove thought of Verena, the first guardian of Rejerrah, who had seen this tree planted by the husband whom she had loved but who had so publicly betrayed her trust.

Dove closed her eyes and saw her grandmother, greying hair piled in coils as plump and smooth as metal, skimming ears from which depended gold and amethyst earrings. The amethysts mirrored the colour of Verena's eyes, so black, so round and glittering and angry that they were shadowed in the same purple hue as the stones in her ears. There was someone else in the room besides Verena but Dove didn't know who it was, nor could she distinguish a voice, but she remembered with a vividness that denied the passage of time, Verena's hand, dark skinned, freckled, flying to her throat, covering the gold bar which she wore across the lace modesty vest at the neck of her pale silk blouse. Dove heard clearly the familiar words which had passed into family legend,

'*How could he behave like that again, it's such ... such impudence.*'

Was that all it was then, Dove wondered? Impudence? A schoolchild was impudent, a puppy, a wine perhaps; but a husband? Dove knew, although she had never understood how she knew, that Verena had been talking of Matabele Jack. The memory was flawed though, incomplete, with no real beginning, and ending abruptly with the word, '*impudence*', spoken as if it had rested reluctantly in her grandmother's mouth.

Dove pieced together her childhood by such memories: tiny fragments of time before her father died; snatches of hushed backstairs gossip when Gracie Beckerleg no longer came to Rejerrah; vignettes of life with her grandparents during the war when Maisie had been away so much of the time. It was only when Lawry and Dove and Maisie were together again that Dove's memory became continuous, and many of the things that had been important before then now took a lesser part, becoming overlaid with shared daily experience.

As she grew older Dove thought about the past more often, scenes like the one that she remembered now returning so vividly that she wondered how much that she believed to be true was indeed so, how much imagination. Had Verena really been wearing a soft grey jacket over a skirt of grey and black stripes, woven and blurred together so that only on close inspection could a distinction be seen between the colours? Had her blouse been cream, the collar corded with rows of tiny, hand-run stitches? Probably, because that was how she always dressed; with shoes of glacé kid for everyday and a narrow handbag of a strange, pockmarked leather which Maisie said was ostrich skin.

Verena had become remote, unpredictable, as she became old, her formidable nature disguised less needfully beneath a mannered and disarming vagueness. Dove understood that she was more like her grandmother than she had ever been like Maisie and by the time she levered herself reluctantly from the bench beneath Matabele Jack's Robinia tree resolution had entered Dove Courtney's soul.

Walking towards the house Dove startled Pender with the warmth of her greeting, quite frightening Sandy caught cocking his leg against an urn of winter pansies in a part of the garden well understood to be forbidden to him.

9

'Three large quiches, do you think, or four?'

'Oh four, Dove always makes enough to feed the five thousand. Little meat patties; *lots* of asparagus in brown bread . . .'

'. . . Scotch eggs made with Bethan's quail's eggs; perhaps a hot dish as it's winter?'

'Sausage rolls, of course, although she *will* use puff pastry and it breaks up and makes such a mess over everything; good paté and cheese, and chicken's legs.'

'Or wings.'

'Oh I do hope it's legs, there was nothing to get hold of in those wings last time and I thought the coating rather odd, made my mouth burn. One thing though, absolutely no one makes better puddings than Dove.'

'I take it we shall accept then?' Enid and Girlie sat over breakfast, their invitations to Dove's party having arrived in the morning post. 'It's odd we haven't so much as glimpsed the new Mrs Eustace, don't you think? And I have a distinct impression that Maisie has been less than her usual unguarded self this last little while. She always gets that sort of lisp when she's prevaricating – always knew when she was, even when we were girls.'

Girlie looked at Enid and smiled her crooked smile. 'I'm sure you're right and Dove was really very disconcerted to see us in Truro, wasn't she? I wonder what's going on at Rejerrah.'

'With wretched Pender so tied up with that little blonde piece he's got his eye on we're missing out on our usual communiqués.'

'Gossip, you mean.'

'Not necessarily; just an intelligent interest in our friends' affairs. And talking of affairs, there *is* something I overheard that I've been saving up to tell you.' Enid spread lime marmalade very slowly on a slice of toast as if mimicking the diffusion of the small amount of news she was offering Girlie. Girlie waited patiently, anticipating what Enid would say but disinclined to diminish her friend's enjoyment of the moment.

'It was when I left you with that new physiotherapist yesterday – reluctantly I can tell you as she looks about fourteen, but then they all do these days. I suppose she's qualified?'

'Of course she is. Don't be so maddening, Enid, what did you hear?'

'I couldn't face the plastic beaker from the machine so I went to that new place in Bread Street. I wanted to see what it's like but it's the same as most of those arty-farty places – nearly broke a crown on the flapjack although the coffee's goodish. Anyway, I was tucked away by a palm tree in the corner behind the door so that I could keep an eye on my umbrella in the stand – I'm still sure that Cissy Beckerleg stole my last one you know, Girlie – when who should come in but Eileen Christopher and Sybil Bauer. You know how loud Sybil is even when she's sober and by then she was well away. Good job the place was empty because she was telling Eileen, at the top of her voice mind you, about Anita Fielding having left her husband and having been taken in by what she referred to as "her sugar daddy".'

Enid sat back and looked at Girlie. 'What d'you think of that? I assumed that Sybil meant poor old Pender, but she went on shrieking for anyone to hear – and this is the worst bit – "that po-faced Dove Courtney's husband. The Welshman with the big nose." Then Eileen said, "Well you know what they say about men with big noses." And they both laughed in an extremely coarse fashion so I paid my bill p d q and slipped out before they could see me.' Enid took such a ferocious bite out of her slice of toast that Girlie feared anew for her crown but Enid went on, 'Do you think it could be true, Girlie? *Lewis*? He's just about the most married man I know.'

'Perhaps that's the trouble, and it might account for Maisie's odd mood lately. But I don't like to think of it, Enid, not *Lewis*. Besides, I wouldn't believe anything those two harpies say; Sybil Bauer is the most vicious gossip I know.' Girlie's hand was shaking so much that waves of tea spilled from the sides of her cup, slopping into the saucer and sprinkling the tablecloth. Enid reached over to steady her, dabbing at the worst of the mess with a bunch of tissues torn from a box on the sideboard.

'How do you suppose Sybil and Eileen knew about Anita Fielding?'

'Don't Eileen's husband and Leo Bauer play golf with what's-his-name Trundell?'

'Denis.'

'Denis Trundell, that's right: and he belongs to the Yacht Club where Anita Fielding worked for a while so he'd have known what was going on and I suppose he told them – you know men can't resist a bit of gossip, especially if it involves a younger woman and an older man. Vicarious enjoyment, I suppose; makes them all feel like young dogs again.'

Enid smirked. 'My mother likened the training of men to that of dogs, you know. She used to say, "Never let them up on the furniture or they get above themselves," and, God knows, she should have known if anyone did.' She tossed the tissues on to an empty plate and stood up to fetch another cup and saucer from the kitchen. When she got back Girlie was more composed.

'I don't know any more than you, Enid, but I did suspect that something of which we weren't altogether aware was going on. That it concerned Lewis hadn't crossed my mind and although Pender may have a weakness in that direction he's always . . .' Girlie stopped.

'Always what?'

'I don't quite know how to put this. What I mean is, Pender's always had certain *standards*, shall we say. What most people don't understand about him is that he likes women he can talk to. Intelligent women.'

'*I* understand that. I always enjoyed sparring with him, but I was much too plain for him to be interested in me in any other way. He does like his women's intellect to be gift-wrapped, wouldn't you say?'

'Oh, Enid, of course, he *is* a man.' Girlie accepted another cup of tea, smiling away Enid's concern as she drank carefully and put the cup down, quite under control once more. 'I believe, now that I think about it, that Pender must have been covering for Lewis and whether that was out of altruism or self-interest we shall have to wait to find out. Perhaps at this party.' Girlie indicated the stiff white At Home cards on the table.

'You never thought of marrying him yourself?'

'Pender? Oh I thought about it, and in many ways he'd have made a better husband than Grenfell ever would, I realise that. Much more fun, except that he *is* such an old woman.'

'At least he's house-trained, Girlie, you can take him anywhere.'

'That's perfectly true, but he'd have fallen to pieces if he hadn't had Maisie and Dove shoring him up all the time.'

'I suppose,' Enid said, 'that's why most men seem to marry again indecently soon when their wife's fallen off the twig. They don't seem to have the what – mettle? Courage, perhaps, to manage on their own. You certainly meet more widows than men on their own wherever you go. And that reminds me, Girlie,' Enid was collecting the plates together, 'I saw that old man who used to live on the corner of Alma Place where that necromancer opened what he likes to call a surgery . . .'

'Mr Roskear. And Paul, I forget what his other name is, is a chiropractor and it *is* a surgery.'

'Necromancer, chiropractor, they're all the same, New Age rubbish.' Enid Glazzard, for whom a dose of salts and two aspirin constituted a remedy for all ills, dismissed the therapist out of hand. 'Yes, Mr Roskear. He was in front of me in the newsagents paying his bill and his trousers were sewn up all down the back seam with huge white stitches. I've seen turkeys trussed up more neatly than that.' Enid carried the plates through to the kitchen and came back with a tray on which she put the tea pot and milk jug and the jars of marmalade and cherry jam. 'That's not why I'm telling you though. It was because the *seam* itself was stained dark brown all the way down. I could hardly bear to look, it made me feel so queasy.'

'How sad. He used to be so dapper in his blazer and white trousers on the bowling green. Poor man, I did hear that his wife had died and I suppose he's let himself go.' Girlie was genuinely sorry for old Mr Roskear in his dirty and badly mended trousers but Enid was impatient.

'That's just what I mean. Who do you know who would go out wearing a stained dress? Not just ordinary dirt; clean dirt, from gardening or decorating or something sensible, but real filth.' She gathered up the cloth, yellow and white seersucker which needed no ironing, shaking the crumbs out of the window to fall into the bright little yard of the garden flat at the back of the house. 'No one! Lots of our friends are widows or live alone but I can't think of anyone at all who'd go out looking like that.

'Although I had so many brothers I've never understood them as a species but I'll tell you one thing, Girlie; when I look around and see old men, I'm always thankful that I'm not married.'

Girlie Eustace looked fondly at her friend. 'You know, Enid, I believe you've discovered the secret at last.'

'Am I supposed to guess, or are you going to tell me what this secret is?' Enid turned from the window, the tea-stained cloth bundled in her arms.

'It was something Verena told me after Matabele Jack died. Grenfell had been dead for nearly ten years by then and everyone had expected me to marry once I got over losing him but, of course, I never did.'

'Never got over Grenfell, you mean?'

Girlie reached forward and with her good hand tried to pull a chair from under the table. Enid completed the move for her and sat down again. 'Of course I did get over him eventually – at least enough for life to become tolerable, but inside, in my heart I suppose you'd have to call it, I still thought of him as my destiny, my children's father, my future.'

'It's not as if you didn't have plenty of other chances is it, particularly when you worked at the WVS canteen? All those big, handsome Americans who wanted to take you back to Texas or California or somewhere. Wasn't there even one from Dakota?'

'Imagine the winters in Dakota! It was bad enough that time I was snowed in when I went to Scotland: I couldn't have stood it for long in Dakota.'

Girlie and Enid were avid readers of the *National Geographic Magazine*, a subscription to which Maisie gave them every year as a joint Christmas present. For two women in whom any change of routine other than the most minimal induced turmoil of a kind agreed to be unwarranted, their armchair excursions into the minutiae of everyday life in some of the most hostile regions of the world was a paradox which intrigued others as well as Maisie. Sometimes their conversation became a surreal mixture of the known and the speculative; the imagined and surmised more exciting than life within the walls of Girlie's prettily decorated flat.

'Are you telling me that you really *never* got over Grenfell Woodvine's death, not in a way that left you free to fall in love with someone else?' Enid, whose romantic experiences had been prosaic and often necessarily secretive, looked at Girlie in astonishment. 'It sounds like something from *Peg's Paper*, for goodness' sake. I know you had several little adventures, as you call them, but what about Pender? He's been your devoted slave for as long as I can remember. You can't tell me that you don't feel anything for him.'

'Of course I do. I love Pender dearly, you know that, but I've never been *in love* with him.' Girlie's lopsided face appeared emotionless and Enid had to listen to her voice to understand what she was trying to convey. 'When Grenfell died I wanted to die too, but I had my war work at the canteen and it seemed so self-indulgent to give in when all those men were in such jeopardy themselves. I just slogged on and gradually it got easier to get up in the morning and slap on the make-up and a smile. Oh, I know that people thought I was just a silly, empty headed little woman and that I'd soon forget, but Verena knew the truth.'

'And this secret she told you?'

'I'm coming to that, but first there's something I have to tell you, Enid, and it's all part of the same thing.' Girlie struggled to her feet. 'I'm sorry, but I need to go to the loo.' The two women walked down the raspberry-carpeted hall towards the bathroom: one pair of legs fragile and bruised looking in flat, sensible slippers with a firm sole; one pair, well-muscled and surprisingly shapely in sheepskin moccasins. When Enid had rearranged Girlie's skirt and washed her hands, they went back, not to the dining room but to the small room decorated in blue and buttery cream which Girlie laughingly called her *boudoir*. The yellow spines of the *Geographic* filled nearly a shelf in the bookcase, now no more than picture books to Girlie Eustace as one of the curious things about her stroke was that it had left her unable to read anything other than that which she had written herself. Girlie looked at the pictures and Enid read the text of the articles aloud to her. They had managed to conceal this disability from almost everyone as the markings on a pack of cards had proved no impediment to Girlie's ability to play. Maisie knew, of course, and Pender, but not those of their acquaintances who made up the circle of bridge players with whom they spent so many afternoons. It was quiet in the placid room, rather too hot: as Girlie felt the cold the radiator was always left on high in here as she liked to sit by the window and look out over the road. It was busy enough to be interesting but there were always parking spaces for Enid's car and with double glazing at all the windows little sound reached the flat. Girlie watched girls walking to school in the morning, grey and green uniforms still the same as Dove and all her friends had worn: a few boys now which Girlie thought odd. Later there were mothers with pushchairs and toddlers, naughty and beautiful, on their way to the nursery school around the corner. She enjoyed the continuity and although she would have liked children of her own, it was one of the sacrifices that Girlie had accepted when she had decided not to marry.

'I decided not to marry, you see.' Girlie looked at Enid. 'It wasn't *because* of what Verena said, but what she said helped to make sense of what I felt.'

Enid was thinking of the breakfast dishes and the laundry that needed to be separated into a dark wash and a white one. There was washing every day, of course, and shopping, and visits to the physio. There were few days when the two women didn't go out at some time and occasionally it was a bit of a scramble to fit everything in. Better that way though, thought Enid, than sitting around feeling sorry for ourselves.

'Sorry, Girlie, what did you say?'

'I said that I decided quite deliberately never to marry. So many people were coming back from the war and getting divorced after disastrous, hasty marriages and sometimes there were children – it was all such a mess.'

'I remember. But Lewis is so overwhelmingly married.' Enid was still thinking of the overheard conversation and Girlie changed tack to accommodate her.

'Imagine what it must be like being married to Rejerrah.'

'See what you mean: at least I think I do. But that doesn't make it any better does it? I can imagine being married to Dove is pretty challenging, but they always seemed so well-suited.'

'Who knows? Maisie probably does but I suspect she will do nothing to jeopardise her own position. That sounds awful and I'm being unfair.' The telephone rang in another part of the flat but neither woman went to answer it. 'Maisie would try to protect Dove from hurt I'm sure, but she would think of herself and Pender too. What would happen to them? Carwarthen, like poor old Ruby? I can't see it somehow.'

'Perhaps it won't come to anything. We've only that vile Sybil's word for it and I just can't see Lewis Courtney going off the rails.' Enid looked at Girlie, smiling faintly. 'For one thing, Dove would never allow it.' There was the complicity of years of friendship and understanding in their laughter.

'Oh Enid, if it weren't for you I'd probably be in Carwarthen myself.'

Girlie's eyes became limpid with emotional tears and Enid said brusquely, 'Oh do shut up, Girlie, you know I'm no good at that sort of stuff.'

'Can't always help it these days, my dear. I don't mean to embarrass you but I did say that there's something I wanted to tell you.' Girlie stopped, looking so tired that Enid was alarmed. 'Don't look so worried,' Girlie said gently, 'I hope it's something that will please you; the best way I can thank you for the way you've looked after me, although nothing can really do that.' Enid tried to speak but Girlie put out a restraining hand and as she moved, a faint whisper of Chanel drifted with her. 'I spoke to Stuart Symons this week and tied up all the loose ends: I've left this flat to you, and you and Pender will share the money. There's plenty – enough for both of you.'

'For goodness' sake, Girlie, why are you telling me this now? I don't want to hear it.' Enid was genuinely agitated.

Girlie Eustace looked at the woman opposite her. 'Living the way we do, with me in this state, we've few secrets from each other and you know as well as I do that I'm not getting any better.' Girlie's two falls, her increasing inability to find the name she wanted quickly enough to satisfy her, her incontinence, underlined the truth that friendship would conceal.

'But you're not *ill*, just need a bit more of a helping hand, that's all.'

Girlie closed her eyes briefly. 'I'm tired, Enid, that's the truth of it. Tired of having to make such an effort at normality all the time and it won't be long before people start noticing my stroke and lose sight of me, Girlie Eustace, spinster of this parish, and I couldn't bear that. Now,' Girlie was brisk again, 'I want you to use some of your money to travel. Go to those places we've read about; go and see them for me. I'd never have gone even when I could have done because I'm much too spoiled – I'd have hated the discomfort. But you're different, Enid, you're made for adventure.'

'I don't want to hear any more of this nonsense. It's not like you and I won't indulge you.' Enid stood up. 'I've got the washing to put in and I promised to 'phone Kevin about the car – it's due for its MOT next week.'

'Don't you want to know the secret that Verena told me?'

'No I don't, if it's more maudlin rubbish.' Enid stumped to the door but turned at the last moment, an almost mischievous expression on her face. 'You can tell me one thing, though.'

'Anything, if I can.'

'What *do* people say about men with big noses?'

Girlie began to laugh, a small hiccupping sound, tension dispersed. 'All those brothers and you really don't know?' Enid shook her head and Girlie said, 'I believe it's the same as they say about men with big feet.'

'Oh, that.' Enid Glazzard, satisfied, closed the door gently behind her, shutting out the truth that Girlie had spoken, erecting a barricade that Enid would defend as long as she was able. She couldn't bear to think of life without Girlie Eustace.

Pender settled down with a drink, *The Cornishman* and a nugget of gentle speculation with which to interest Maisie. Sandy was asleep in his creaking basket under the desk and Pender had that afternoon successfully negotiated the swop of some seeds of a hollyhock almost as dark as chocolate which he had coveted for months. He was a happy man.

He studied the obituaries in the newspaper: every line,

from the name of the deceased, most of whom he recognised, to the last self-consciously dignified message on a wreath. He noted the names of the chosen bearers and who had represented those unable to be present, reading aloud to Maisie verses of sincere regret but inexpert composition which filled the columns. 'I see Charlie Blight's been busy this week; his name's down here three times. At this rate I shall have to review his handicap as he'll soon overtake Sid Pollard as Penalverne's universal mourner.'

'It seems like a fairly harmless hobby to me. Gets him out of the house and gives him a feed once or twice a week.'

Pender chuckled and read on. 'Didn't know that man who was an expert on old Cornish dialect was dead, did you?'

'*I* did: I remembered because he had an unusual name.'

'Darcy Jose, and only seventy-five. Seems to me that more and more knowledge of old Cornwall's going up the flue at Penmount every year.' Pender returned to *The Cornishman* and the reports from the Women's Institutes, which he read with the same facetious attention he had given to the obituaries, before refilling his glass and settling down to the full page advertisement for Trago Mills.

Maisie was knitting basket-weave squares in fluorescent orange and cobalt blue woven with a rainbow coloured fleck. The effect was unappealing but she was using wool donated to St John Bosco's and left in a box in the church porch following an appeal for the missions. Maisie thought the colours might suit dark skins better than pale English ones, doing her best to make them less repellant by the skill of her workmanship. Maisie thought of Ruby Eustace in Carwarthen and the bewilderment with which she herself had watched several old women unpicking their knitting at the end of visiting time, lengths of crinkled and frayed yarn wound slowly round old, dry fingers into over tight balls in an effort to return it to some sort of useable condition.

Ruby had seen her expression and had cackled with laughter. 'They only have a ball or two so they have to use it over and over. I'm all right because Girlie brings me as much as I want.' Her blunt hands flew along the rows and her voice became gracious. 'It was good of you to bring me some wool, Maisie, but I shall have to swap it for something mauveish. Mauveish, mauver, mauve; mauve, mauver, mauvest,' she sang under her breath, having quite forgotten her visitors, heavy crop-haired head bent over her work. Maisie had left the communal sitting room thankfully: it was full of the noise of a television which no one watched but which was never turned off between breakfast and bedtime. The poignant sight of women who had knitted and sewed for children and grandchildren now just sitting and forlornly unravelling wool to be used again the next day had stayed with her for a very long time.

Now Maisie finished aloud one of those silent conversations she held with herself these days. Pender, better able than most to interpret the significance of her words, looked at her over the top of his newspaper. 'You won't let them send me there will you, Pen darling?'

'Where? And who's going to send you there?'

'Carwarthen. And Dove, if she sells the house.'

'Why the hell should she want to sell Rejerrah?' Pender was startled. 'Unless she's said something to you that I don't know about.' He lowered *The Cornishman* into his lap, keeping his finger between the pages reporting the rugby matches and scores and looked towards his sister. 'Actually, old thing, I was going to tell you – Dove was in remarkably good spirits when I saw her a little while ago. She *nearly*, not *quite* but *very* nearly, patted Sandy on the head and considering what he was doing at the time it came as quite a surprise. And she gave me a very chipper greeting – alarmed both of us, I can tell you.'

'I'm surprised to hear that because she was very down

this morning. I wonder what's happened since then.' Maisie changed from cobalt blue wool to orange, picking shreds of glittering rainbow plastic from her lap. 'You don't think she could possibly have guessed about Lewis, do you? I ask because I'm sure that Jossy knows and probably Diana, too, by now. And if they know, the chances are that Dove does as well.'

'That would hardly cheer her up, would it? And all the diversionary tactics I've been engaged in – gone for nothing . . .'

'. . . And it's not as if you took any pleasure in Mrs Fielding's company, after all.'

Pender looked at his sister who met his eyes with an expression of such innocence and lack of guile that it made Pender laugh. 'Don't mind about her too much, although ten years ago . . . Well, what I mean to say,' he closed the newspaper, folding each corner exactly on top of the one below, aligning the middle sheets where they had slipped down in his grasp, 'I shall miss that little chap, Cody. Daft bloody name but he's a little cracker, notwithstanding.' He cleared his throat and took a sip from his whisky. 'Haven't told me yet why you think Dove might sell Rejerrah.'

'Well, if she divorces Lewis, she might go and live in a commune like Bethan or a cottage somewhere and take up jewellery making or aromatherapy. I read about it all the time: women of a certain age who find themselves and start a new life. Probably find herself a toy boy as well – and then where will we all be?'

'This won't do, Maisie.' Pender spoke firmly. 'Noticed you've been a bit inclined to the doleful lately, old thing. Got to guard against the mawkish; don't even let it creep into your mind. I never do and things have worked out for me, can't say they haven't.' Maisie Eustace, being a kind woman and fond of her brother, allowed Pender to continue in his delusion that his present comfortable circumstances had been achieved by his own application and ability. In truth, a certain shrewdness, a resourcefulness honed from years of living on his charm, had contributed to his prevailing contentment but if Pender Woodvine understood that it was because of his niece's sense of duty and his sister's accommodating memory that he lived in complacent retirement at Rejerrah, he had decided to disregard it. He felt that he had always made his contribution by his optimistic presence and his ability to enliven the most tedious of daily routines. 'Can't see Dove ever letting go of Rejerrah; not in her nature to let go of anything belonging to her. Speaking of which, she won't let Lewis go, you know. Tooth and nail, all that sort of thing.'

Pender stood up. 'Come on, Maisie, I'm taking you out to dinner. Can't stand watching you knitting that God-awful stuff all evening. What'll it be? Fish and chips or Chinese?'

'I'll think about it while I tidy myself up a bit. Will you set the video for me for *Coronation Street*? Channel three at seven thirty.' Maisie went to her bedroom knowing quite well that Pender was incapable of correctly setting any video recorder and how astonished he would be to find a programme about antiques on the tape when they returned. Maisie would telephone Enid in the morning for an update on the story.

Outside it was raining; slanting Cornish rain which dampened everything without ever soaking it; glossing the grey slabs and laying down foundation for a new generation of lichen and moss to grow on roof and stone and tree trunk. Pender went to fetch the Princess and to drive her nearer the house so that Maisie had only a few steps to walk in the rain. As he approached the garage he was surprised to see Dove at the bottom of the steps that led to the flat above. Too late to turn back, Pender waved and raised his voice. 'Taking Maisie out for supper – Lotus Garden, I expect. Touch of the old sweet and sour do her good.'

Pender started to hum, 'We're off to Chez Maxim's' and Dove smiled saying only, 'Enjoy yourselves,' before continuing to climb upwards to Anita Fielding's two rooms. Pender tried to watch the women greeting each other but saw only a triangle of light as the door was opened, rain suspended in the glow, neither falling nor forming drops; light, annoying rain that made the windscreen wipers drag smearily across the glass, but without which he couldn't see well enough to drive.

Maisie had tied a pink chiffon scarf over her hair and she settled in the front of the Princess. 'Shall we go to the Lotus Garden? Enid said the lemon chicken there was quite delish and I'd like to try it. And noodles of course.'

'Oodles of noodles.' Pender smiled; his sister's late-flowering passion for Chinese food still amused him, and Maisie's boldness in ordering dishes which were unknown to her.

There was nowhere to park very near the restaurant so Pender stopped outside and Maisie got out of the car. By the time he had walked back from the side street where he had left the Princess, Maisie was sitting at a table studying the menu. They ordered and picked at prawn crackers while they waited for the crabmeat soup. 'Saw Dove as I went for the Princess, going up to Anita Fielding's.'

'Actually into the flat?'

'Looked like it. Have you ordered Jasmine tea?'

'Of course. I don't like it, Pender.'

'Then why did you order it? Besides, I thought you enjoyed it.'

'Not the tea.' Maisie sounded impatient. 'Dove going to see Anita Fielding. Does that mean that she *does* know or that she *doesn't*? I *hate* this sort of thing, Pender. It's all wrong and there are those two children as well. Whatever was Lewis thinking of?'

'No excuse, I know, but I'd got a bit too involved with the dazzling Anita and Lewis was actually trying to help me extricate myself after I realised that her husband was thirty years younger than me and about two foot taller.' The soup arrived and for a while there was silence. 'I'd told her that if she had to leave him I might be able to help her find a place, never thinking *for a moment* that she'd take me up on it, so when she did, Lewis tried to explain to her that it wasn't actually on.'

'And?'

'And, I'm afraid, somewhere along the line, he fell for her. I think he just felt sorry for her at first but things got out of hand and . . . well, you know how it happens.' The soup bowls were removed, replaced by two chafing dishes with nightlights shining through their silver fretwork tops.

'I'm not at all sure that I *do* know how it happens – and is it still going on? Under my daughter's nose; in the flat my daughter has, out of the goodness of her heart, lent her?'

'I'm not sure, Maisie, and that's the truth. May I try your lemon chicken?' Maisie pushed the bowl towards Pender and he helped himself to meat and sauce. 'Not sure, though, about out of the goodness of Dove's heart. I understood it was the lesser of two evils: Anita and children or Lawry and Loretta. Good this, isn't it? But, on balance, I think I prefer the chicken with cashew nuts – what about you? Meet expectations?'

'It's very good.' Maisie refilled her bowl and ate in silence. She wasn't able to manage chopsticks and used a fork and a spoon. After a while she said, 'I'm not naive enough to believe Dove immune from deception but she really doesn't deserve it you know, Pen. Even though she's my own daughter I know that she's a good person: someone who would never deliberately choose to do anything she perceived as wrong, and someone who does actively try to do the right thing.'

'I know, old girl, I know. But so does Lewis; he's been a good father and the best husband he knows how to be. Or at least that's the way I see it,' Pender added, his opinions often tempered by caution, qualified by knowing that they were welcome only as long as they remained appropriate. It was Dove who had made this very clear to him but that was something which Pender would never discuss with Maisie; the humiliation of suppressing his views on many things the price he paid for a roof over his head and the ability to take his rightful place in Penalverne society.

'I suppose it's sex: Lewis *is* Welsh, after all.'

'Extraordinary thing to say!' Pender sat back and looked across the table at his sister. 'What's being Welsh got to do with it?' He started to laugh. 'You know, Maisie, you can still surprise me, even at our age.'

'Verena would never employ a Welsh girl, had you forgotten? She said they were much too pretty and much too sexy. She had a theory that it was because so many of the Welsh had suffered from tuberculosis and it was somehow connected in her mind with excessive sexual appetites.'

'The medicine they took, I believe. But Verena'd never use a word like sexy.'

'What she actually said was that they all had a come-hither look in their eyes that enticed men to lust.'

'That sounds more like the dear old mum – at least she'd learned something from being married to Matabele Jack.' Pender scraped the last of the rice, coloured with flecks of scrambled egg and now rather cold, on to his plate and smiled at Maisie. 'So, instead, she employed Gracie Beckerleg, who looked like something that'd been left out in the rain and forgotten. That, as Cody would say, is good thinking.'

'You really are fond of him, aren't you?'

Pender refused to be drawn. 'Lychees?'

Maisie shook her head. 'I've had enough, thank you: and thank you for bringing me out, I've enjoyed it.'

Pender was hesitant. 'You don't seem to have been out as much as usual lately. No problem with Girlie or Enid, is there?' He looked keenly at Maisie and she sighed and laid her napkin on the table.

'No, of course not. There's just so much going on at the moment and I feel I have to be on hand in case I'm needed. As if I'd make any difference – a dotty old woman like me.' She laughed, screwing up her face. 'I just feel that they're all *safer* if I'm there.'

'And you don't have to worry about letting anything indiscreet slip out.' The words were spoken lightly, Pender's eyes on his plate.

'You know me too well for me to be able to get away with anything. I'm afraid of making matters worse, that's the truth; either between Dove and Lewis or Dove and Loretta or, oh Lord, Dove and Anita Fielding. There, I've said it and it sounds worse aloud than it did in my head.'

'All I heard was a catalogue of Dove's little local difficulties, nothing to do with you at all. You're not going to be able to stop whatever is inevitable from happening, Maisie my dear, so I think you should forget about it all and ring Girlie tomorrow and fix something up. I could take us all out for a run if you like: lunch in St Just, perhaps, but you'll have to pay as I am, as usual, not overly burdened with the old spondoolics.'

The bill came and Maisie resisted the temptation to gather it up and pay for their meal. Darren Wang, born and bred in Penalverne, handed her a carnation in a twist of cellophane as they left the restaurant and Maisie was absurdly pleased with this gesture, holding it gently until she should reach home and could find the right vase to display the flower to advantage.

10

Jossy scooped the final batch of Scotch eggs from the saucepan of oil, letting them drain for a minute before laying them carefully on a wodge of kitchen paper which absorbed the last of the grease. She crossed *Scotch eggs* off the list stuck to a cupboard door and let her eyes drift over Dove's detailed instructions to find her next task, settling on *Pea and mint soup: make – leave in saucepan – DO NOT use aluminium.*

'Are you sure about this soup, Loretta? It sounds to me more like a picnic thing for the summer. I could make leek and potato or something.'

Loretta looked up from the table where she was splitting dates carefully down the middle, extracting the stone and refilling the void with marzipan. 'Quite sure, Jossy. Your mother chose it after careful thought and it was always a great favourite . . .' she stopped, retrieved a date stone which had skittered to the floor, and went on, '. . . where I used to live.'

'Hawthorn Lodge, you mean?' Loretta nodded, not meeting Jossy's eye.

'Well, if you're sure, but it still seems a funny choice to me.' Jossy sat down, pushing damp hair off her forehead, scraping the thin grey membrane from a stone with her teeth like a small beaver. 'Shall I make coffee while you finish what you're doing? I don't know about you but I'm flagging a bit.'

'I could do with a drink.' Loretta smiled. 'But I'm enjoying doing this, you know, although I'm surprised your mother trusts us to manage without supervision. I thought Dove would want to be in charge of all the preparations herself.'

'I expect she would really, so just be thankful that she's not feeling well.' Jossy poured water into the filter and the smell of the Fair Trade coffee she had bought in an Oxfam shop filled the kitchen. She sat down watching the pale drops splash out of the dark sludge in the paper cone. 'That was a rotten thing to say and I didn't mean it because Mum's migraines make her really ill and this one seems worse than most.' Jossy topped up the filter then said, 'Loretta?'

'Yes.' Loretta was washing the sticky mess of dates off her fingers, careful to remove every scale which stuck as though glued to her skin. When she was satisfied she dried her hands, arranged the towel with care on the hook and sat down opposite Jossy. 'Yes, Jossy, what is it?'

'You mustn't mind Mum, you know.' The words left a space in Jossy's chest that made her feel unbalanced, as if the thought had a physical manifestation, the dissipation of which had left her incomplete. 'She does her best and she does have a lot to put up with from all of us. It's just that sometimes she wants things to be better than they are. I think she's afraid that people will feel let down if something's not very good and she tries to make sure that everything's as perfect as it can be.'

Loretta's eyes were fixed on Jossy, watching her unwaveringly as the girl tried to find words to lessen the distance between her mother and her uncle's unfamiliar and candid new wife.

'Who expects things to be perfect?' Loretta poured coffee

into two mugs, fetching the milk jug which she put down by Jossy. 'I certainly don't. Do you? Do you expect perfection, Jossy?'

'No, of course I don't: nor does my mother. She just *wants* things to be . . . right, I think.'

Loretta looked as if she were counting the grains of sugar in the bowl in front of her, her extraordinary concentration diverted from Dove towards something more immediate. Jossy decided to say no more and was startled when Loretta looked up and said in a conversational voice, 'That's why she drives people away. No one wants to be thought not up to standard, judged to be second best.' Jossy felt panicky and wished she had never started the conversation. She might have carried such thoughts half-formed in her own mind, but she would never have spoken them aloud. Loretta was still watching her, no sound at all in the old-fashioned, echoing kitchen, except the clicking of the defective clock on the cooker and the slow drip of a tap which Lewis had been promising for weeks to mend.

Jossy thought of Diana, who even now was planning to go to London; to find a job and a flat where she could be anonymous, away from her mother's exaggerated and barely concealed expectation of a reconciliation with Luke. She thought of Bethan; silly, loyal Bethan, the most easily influenced of all of them but who had left home rather than allow Dove to demand more devotion than she could ever generate. As for Lewis . . . Jossy shook her head to dislodge any thought of her father from her mind, as if the physical action would silence those insistent voices which taunted her with the knowledge she found so perilous.

Loretta understood that shake of denial very well and she spoke to Jossy again. 'Until I met your Uncle Lawry I was always sub-standard, you see: *NOT QUITE PERFECT* as they put on the towels and sheets we had in the place where I used to live. I was never sure if it referred to the linen or to us but it always seemed entirely appropriate to me.' She smiled an engaging smile that softened her pale face and showed off her excellent teeth. 'Lawry's still perceived as NQP by a lot of people, including your mother, so perhaps that's why we suit each other so well – sharing our obvious imperfections.' Loretta poured herself another half-cup of coffee, noticing that Jossy hadn't even touched hers. 'Drink your coffee, Joss.'

The girl drank automatically, then looked at Loretta. She almost whispered, 'You see Mummy thinks, she truly *believes*, that she's making everyone's life better: that by taking everything on herself and by trying to make everything as perfect as possible, she's improving our lives, and she's *not* and I just want her to *stop*: I want her do what *she* wants and leave us alone to do what we want: to be what we are.'

'To go to hell in a handcart in your own way, you mean?'

Jossy nodded, tears glittering in her eyes. Loretta was matter-of-fact, 'I think she *is* doing what she wants and perhaps you have to learn to accept that. It could be,' Loretta said, 'that you have to distance yourself as your sisters have done.' The drip from the tap became insistent and she got up to turn it off more tightly, damaging the washer even further. She turned around and looked at Jossy. 'And just as your father is doing.'

Now Jossy's tears slid down her cheeks quite silently as if they were as solid as crystal; as if they should have been caught and held forever in a lachrymatory to mark the day she had relinquished childhood to this strange, pale woman who spoke the words that no one else would dare to say.

Loretta watched Jossy, noticing how her tears shone; how her little apple-cheeked face was as smooth as a child's, the dark skin inherited from Lewis, warm and golden brown. Jossy didn't sob or sniffle but her tears sliding silently from almost black eyes looked sadder for the unconstrained way in which they flowed. Loretta wanted to comfort the girl but she knew that Jossy needed to meet this crisis on her own, reassurance would come later.

Loretta went to the pantry where the vegetables were kept and came back with a large plastic bag, tipping the contents on to the table between them. Jossy, composed again, had fetched two colanders and drew a pile of the out-of-season peas towards her. 'I don't know how Mum can buy these, they're *so* expensive and did you see that programme about how the farmers who grow them are exploited?'

'I thought it was the pickers who were exploited, not the farmers.'

Jossy looked thoughtfully at Loretta before saying, 'You're absolutely right, of course. Do you know, Loretta, I don't understand how anyone thinks that you're dim.' Jossy stopped, her face a picture of confusion. 'Oh, sugar, I shouldn't have said that. Oh, I'm really, really sorry.'

Loretta smiled; her fingers slicing open the pods gathered the too-small peas into a green mound in the colander without wavering. 'Why not? It's true. A lot of people think I'm reckless because I say what I think. *I've* always thought it foolish not to although it can lead to misunderstandings, I grant you that. On the whole though I think it's better to take the chance and speak the truth.'

'Aren't you afraid of hurting people – not everyone wants to hear the truth, do they?'

Loretta's long, thin hand stretched into the mound on the table and she shuffled more peas towards her. Her arm was marked by a white band where her watch strap had shielded the skin from a burning French sun, the tan fading into that ashy yellow which gave her complexion such a curious cast. She looked at Jossy, the quietest, most imposed upon of Dove's daughters and said lightly, 'Untruth hurts as well, you know.'

'I don't understand.'

'Well, if you live in an atmosphere where the truth is unacknowledged; where it's concealed, even; where there is *untruth*, things can happen that are terribly damaging.'

'I suppose so. You don't mean,' Jossy's mouth felt dry but she forced herself to finish. 'Daddy?'

Loretta looked at the girl. 'I wasn't thinking of him particularly, but yes, someone is going to get hurt: they always do in situations like that. In a way, it just underlines the point I was making.'

'What do you mean?'

'Absolutely everyone – Pender, your grandmother and, no doubt, her friends Enid and Girlie, you, all the people surrounding your mother in fact, have been trying to conceal the truth from her about Anita Fielding. Don't you think that if someone had said weeks ago that she was getting too involved with your father, it might never have gone as far as it has? You have all allowed Dove to go on thinking that it was Pender who was smitten with Anita . . .'

'Well, it was – in the beginning.'

'Perhaps it was for a while but even Lawry and I could see what was happening as soon as we arrived here.'

'So why didn't you say something, if you really believe in telling the truth?' Even to Jossy's ears this sounded childish, defensive.

Loretta looked at her. 'I did. I felt I had to speak to Dove about it.'

'Oh.' Jossy considered the foolhardiness of this, quickly understanding the implications. 'She didn't believe you, did she?'

Loretta shook her head, recognising perfectly that it was at that moment of truth that Dove had decided her sister-in-law was a mischief-maker and had made up her mind that from then onwards she would neither make the effort to get to know Loretta, nor accept her.

'Poor Mummy.' Jossy looked as if she were going to cry again and Loretta started to talk.

'You think I might hurt people by telling the truth? Well I want you to understand about *untruth* and how much that can hurt.' The peas were finished before Loretta started her story and she and Jossy sat at the kitchen table, heaps of empty pods between them, a colander of bright green peas in front of each of them.

Loretta looked at her hands stained from the vegetables, the skin under her thumb nail green and sore where she had run it down the tough seam of the pods. 'Just now when I spoke about somewhere I used to live, I allowed you to assume that I meant Hawthorn Lodge. That was wrong of me because it wasn't true. I was talking about somewhere else; a place where, not of my own volition, I was forced to live for several years.' Loretta had linked her fingers together and now flexed her hands, palms upwards as if she were playing the child's game, Here's the church, here's the steeple. Jossy waited. 'It was actually a hospital where I was sent to be cured of telling the truth.'

There was the sound of Jossy's indrawn breath, shuddering slightly from the tears which were still only lightly suppressed. Loretta gave her a sympathetic smile. 'You've no need to worry; I may be judged to be terminally absurd but I'm not mad. I never was: I really never was. Do you know why I was locked away? That's a silly question because of course you don't: you'd never even guess. It was because I told the truth. And because I tried to kill my father.'

'Oh, Loretta.' Jossy's eyes looked huge but as Loretta stared at her, Jossy was unable to hold her gaze and lowered her lids and began to slice through and through an empty pea pod with her nails.

'My mother was a good woman, anyone would tell you that. Always the first to volunteer for anything needing to be done in the parish; flower rota, church cleaning, washing up after meetings, mending hassocks and cassocks and observing all the feasts and fasts assiduously.'

In the silence they heard the sound of a car being driven around to the back of the house and Jossy looked up, hoping no one would interrupt them, but the car stopped short of Rejerrah's back door and several people, laughing together, went in to Maisie's part of the house.

'They see the truth in their own way, too,' Loretta said.

'Who?'

'Maisie, Pender, their friends. They see only what they want to see and by disregarding anything they find unpalatable they do such harm. I've always thought that unconditional loyalty is so misguided: just an excuse not to have to think for yourself really.'

'Oh, no! I don't think you're right, Loretta, I really don't. They're so *kind*, so *nice* to each other – and everyone else.'

'But don't you understand? By *always* being "nice" and "kind", it means that if anyone around them is unhappy or feels that something's wrong, they're not free to do anything about it and they just have to go on pretending that everything's all right. People who've lived such comfortable, indulged lives nearly always have the same philosophy of "just ignore it and it'll go away" – except that it doesn't, of course.'

Jossy looked unconvinced. 'I think,' she said, 'that they're just doing the British thing of keeping a stiff upper lip and making light of trouble. It's the way they were brought up and the only way they know how to go about things.'

Loretta shrugged and went on, 'You're partly right and someone like Pender has had some experience of life outside the confines of this insular little town, but believe me, I know what I'm talking about. My mother was like that: see only the good, ignore the unacceptable, and bad luck if it just happens to be your daughter who is breaking up inside, shattering into so many pieces that not all of them will ever be recovered.'

'But you said it was your father you tried to . . . to . . .' Jossy found it difficult to say the word.

'To kill.' Loretta had no such inhibitions. 'Yes it was, and it was because I had always told the truth about him and no one would listen to me that I had to do something, and when I did the people who wouldn't listen to me before said I was a liar, a troublemaker, an attention seeker. So they put me in a hospital and tried to make me say I had made it all up, but I wouldn't because it was all *true*.'

'I'm a bit muddled: what was it you said your father had done, that no one would believe?'

'I told my mother over and over again that as soon as she went out to meet her sister on Sunday afternoons, my father would take me upstairs and indulge in what is now called inappropriate behaviour.'

'And she didn't believe you?'

Loretta shook her head again. 'I begged my mother to stop him; at least to speak to him, but do you know what she said?' Loretta looked at her hands: Open the door and here are the people. 'She laughed: she actually laughed and said, "When I first met your father he was the handsomest man I'd ever seen." Then she would say she didn't want to hear any more of my lies and go on to talk about who'd been at Benediction and what setting of *Tantum Ergo* they'd used.'

'So,' Jossy said slowly, 'you were living in an atmosphere of *untruth*; an atmosphere of truth denied.'

'Now you're beginning to understand.'

'And what happened, Loretta? What did you do?'

'I tried talking to my aunt but my mother had convinced her that I was making it all up, and there was no one else I could tell – not the nuns and certainly not the priest. Even the doctor was an old friend of my father's and although I did try he never took anything that I said to him seriously. Then one Sunday lunchtime, for some reason, I forgot to put out the big knife and fork my father used to carve the meat and I was sent to fetch them from the sideboard.'

Loretta could see the table, reproduction Georgian with brass feet, polished, dotted with mats of botanical speci-mens – pink-and-white-striped camellias, damask roses, lilies. They had been a present from her aunt to her parents one Christmas and now they were faded, with brown patches showing through where constant scouring was effacing any charm they had ever had. There were covered dishes of roast potatoes and cabbage on the table and a sauce boat of gravy and one of apple sauce. In front of her father's place was a hand-and-spring of pork, far too large a joint for such a small family but which would be used to the last unpalatable scrap in one guise or another until Friday, when dinner would be cod in parsley sauce and boiled potatoes.

Loretta saw herself take the knife and fork out of the drawer in the sideboard and felt again the rough, serrated handles fashioned to look like the antlers of a deer. Was it something in her father's intrusive smile as he stood at the head of the table, or the collusive way her mother ducked her head as she shook out her napkin? Loretta never knew, hardly seeing beyond the meat on the carving dish; know-ing that when the portion allocated for that day's meal had been eaten; when the Bakewell tart and custard that followed had been cleared away, Mrs Lyons would go to wash her hands and find her gloves. As it was summer she would fold a mantilla into her handbag, her unbecoming hat reserved for the colder weather later in the year.

When she had gone the house filled with threat as dense as fog, making Loretta wheeze and struggle for breath. She had cleared the table and washed up and as she hung the dish rag over the tap to dry, her father would be there, contaminating, inevitable.

It had been on the twenty-ninth of June that Loretta Lyons had stepped around the table and instead of placing the carving knife under her father's waiting hand, she had plunged it with all her strength into the middle of his chest. She remembered the date so clearly because her mother had made a fuss about missing Benediction and the start of a special novena to St Peter and St Paul whose feast day it happened to be.

When Loretta had stopped talking Jossy was quiet; not shocked, being a child who had devoured anything in print since she was old enough to make out the headlines in a newspaper, but trying to understand what relevance it had to her own situation. At last she said, 'The bit about your father doesn't really have anything to do with it, does it? It's the fact that no one believed the truth when you told it, and you're trying to persuade me that we should tell the truth, even if people get hurt. The thing is, you see, that I don't think I agree with you. I hate having to hurt people; I think most people do, and that means not always being able to tell the absolute truth.' Jossy looked at the pea pod shredded into ribbons held together by the faded flower at the end of the stalk which she was holding in her hand. She threw it on to the pile in front of her. 'Anyway, I'd have thought that when no one would believe you like that, you'd never bother to be truthful again – just say whatever was easiest.'

'I suppose some people would react like that but the more I was disbelieved, the more determined I became not to lie. Oh, it would have been the easy way out but it became the one way I had of punishing my father. If

I kept on saying the same thing I thought that perhaps, eventually, someone might believe me about him. And, of course,' Loretta said with a small smile, 'I *am* a bit obsessive.'

'What happened to your parents, you know – after?'

'When my father's wound had healed – and it wasn't as bad as it looked at first – he just disappeared and good riddance, I say; I never want to see him again. My mother sold the house and she and her sister went to live in Southampton because they'd discovered there was a church there where Mass was still said in Latin. As far as I know that's where they live now: Benediction three times a week and Mass every morning. That's how it was the last time I saw them anyway.'

'When was that?'

'When I came out of hospital. I had to be discharged into my mother's care but she and Aunt Sheila soon got shot of me, which suited us all very well. I went to work at Hawthorn Lodge and I stayed there until I met your Uncle Lawry.'

'Loretta?'

'Ummh?'

'I'm glad you married Uncle Lawry. I wasn't sure at first but I see now that I'd just accepted my mother's opinion of him and hadn't tried to understand for myself what he's really like. Or you, for that matter.'

'You shouldn't worry about that because Dove *is* very forceful in her opinions, and if you're beginning to understand that it's a start, Jossy. Try to accept that truth isn't always what we want it to be, and sometimes, you know, your mother *is* right. But not about Lawry. And not about me,' Loretta made a cluck of impatience. 'Before we do anything else, I'm going to mend that tap, it's driving me mad; drip, drip, drip.'

'Can you do that too?'

'Oh yes, and I'll teach you how if you'll just show me where the stopcock is.' The two women smiled at each other, Jossy's misgivings about disloyalty to her mother lessened from the distraught arguments she conducted with herself, knowing that Dove's influence had already raised expectations which she, Jossy, could never fulfil. Dove's unrealistic presumption of her daughter's capabilities coloured Jossy's existence; the evidence laid before her Dove chose to ignore, preferring to believe that Jossy would achieve more even than Diana, making up in some way for the disappointment of Bethan's rejection of the established way of life which prevailed at Rejerrah.

'I don't feel like doing any more this morning. Let's leave the puddings until after lunch and perhaps we could get Di to help us, she's always been much better at them than I am. She's a very good cook, you know, but she won't be pressurised into doing what she doesn't want to do and she's terribly anti this party because Mum's invited Luke. It's a waste of time because Diana absolutely won't go back to him but Mummy just *can't* accept that it's over.'

'There, that should do it. Go and turn the water on again, will you?' Loretta replaced the tap. 'Diana's more than capable of looking after herself so let her sort it out with your mother. You just concentrate on doing what you really want, which, if I'm not mistaken, doesn't include going to university.'

'How can you possibly know that?'

'Oh, I've had lots of opportunity to learn how to watch and listen to people. We all say a great deal without actually using any words, you know.' No need, Loretta thought, to tell Jossy that Maisie had let slip this intelligence one evening over what she insisted on calling 'drinkies'. Some mystery, Loretta believed, was always an advantage, even to her.

*   *   *

Dove lay in the darkened bedroom, too nauseous to move more than was unintentional. She had tried lying flat without a pillow; with one; propped almost upright by two, but nothing had helped. The array of sparkling lights which had moved from left to right across her field of vision would have been admirable at a fireworks spectacular but when, for a short time at the height of the manifestation, Dove's vision had been totally obscured, she had felt as if death might be the easy option. She had taken her pills at the first sign of numbness in her tongue; the prickling, tingling sensation in her left cheek preceding the headache which would follow when the pageant of lights had played itself out like some queasy hallucination. The only thing that made it even remotely bearable, Dove thought, was the knowledge that tomorrow she would feel better; weak and washed out but free from pain.

Dove had woken that morning with a tightness at the base of her skull that she had come to dread, knowing that before an hour or two had passed she would be enduring yet another headache which made her long to be insensate.

The day had started badly. Maisie was already up and sitting in a chair when Dove had arrived for her early morning visit. She knew what that meant and while Maisie was captive in her upright, enclosed bath, Dove changed the sheets on the bed, conscious even then of the sensation of being stabbed that made her wince each time she lowered her head. Maisie was contrite, Dove reassuring her that it was no trouble at all and trying to make light of a situation which both of them found distressing. Dove had opened the window, and in doing so had knocked over the painted china boot which stood on the sill. It's padded velvet lining still holding Verena's glass topped pins had fallen out, the old glue as hard and crusty as a scab. Dove had retrieved the pieces and taken them into the sitting room to find a newspaper in which to wrap them, carrying the package through to her own kitchen with the bundle of sheets for the washing machine. Whatever else she did that day, the velvet pad would be reclaimed, reglued, and the boot returned to Maisie almost before she had time to notice its absence.

As she thought about this, Dove remembered that at least she had replaced the empty tube of glue with a new one when she had bought Sellotape and envelopes and coloured paper clips on her last foray into Smith's. Even through the pain in her head Dove smiled to herself, remembering how a small Diana and a smaller Bethan had always referred to the stationers as *WHSmithandSons* as if it had been one word. She thought they had been happy when they were small and now she wondered if Anita Fielding always had spare rubber bands and plenty of stamps because Lewis would hardly know where to go to buy those things which he found indispensable but for which Dove had assumed total liability. She thought of the mauve biro which she had found in her jar of pens on the kitchen dresser, puzzled then as to its provenance but no longer in any doubt as to where it had come from.

When an intrigued Pender had seen Dove on the steps to Anita Fielding's flat he had guessed correctly that she was on a tour of reconnaissance to assess the exact scale of the opposition. This was disguised as a friendly overture and she had been open and affable when she had come upon Freya and Cody lying on the floor, felt pens and crayons around them in a confusion of colour. Dove had noticed the companions of the mauve biro, each slotted into the transparent compartment of a long pencil case as Freya conscientiously returned each pen to its allotted place. That it was Cody who generated the jumble of paper and pens surrounding the children was obvious, Freya as neat and anxious a child as she would become a woman.

Dove had smiled at Freya and Cody who had returned her greeting with the false rictus of obedience affected by children told too often to be polite. They had returned to their colouring books and Dove had said, 'I believe I have one of your pens in my kitchen. If you like to call round you can have it back; I wondered where it had come from.'

'Lewis pinched it and didn't give it back.'

'Be quiet, Cody, you know you're not supposed to talk about Lewis,' Freya hissed, pushing the little boy's arm so that his pen skittered over the outline within which he was colouring. He reached over to scribble on his sister's neat, pallid flowers and she turned, grizzling, to her mother. Dove watched as Anita patiently explained to Cody that his behaviour was unkind and made him apologise, before comforting Freya for the unwanted scarlet scrawl in her picture.

'You could turn it into a lovely bed of *love lies bleeding*,' Anita said and Dove wondered why neither child had been reprimanded as hers would surely have been if they had misbehaved when they were as young as the Fieldings.

When the children were separated and had returned to their colouring there was a silence, Anita apprehensive about Dove's visit, Dove having to reconsider what she would say after hearing her husband's name spoken so familiarly by the small boy at her feet. Anita broke the silence. 'Were your plants OK?' Dove looked at her. 'When your car ran over them?'

'Oh, yes. Thank you.'

'I was sorry about that but Freya's asthma's been really bad lately and the clinic said they'd fit me in if I could come right away. I was trying to turn the radio off as it was a talk about,' she looked towards the two bent heads and said very quietly, 'abortion.'

'I see,' Dove said. 'Yes, I do see. Is Freya better now?'

'A lot better than she was, thanks. I suppose it's not

surprising that the poor little thing's been so bad with all the upsets we've had lately.'

'Quite.' Dove had no intention of pursuing this line of conversation but she remembered why she had come and tried to sound more amiable than she felt. 'Actually I came to bring you this.' She put the invitation in its heavy envelope on the table, which Anita had covered with a sheet of thick plastic patterned with red barns and fields of maize where roguish cows beamed over one spotted shoulder. It was absurd but Dove remembered a nursery where Baby Bunting had prevailed over just such incongruous, frolicking Bunnikins and thought better of Anita Fielding.

Anita was hesitant about opening the envelope, afraid in spite of what Pender had said, that it might be a demand for rent, Dove an alarming, unfamiliar presence of whom Anita was unsure. Lewis spoke of Dove only to praise her; to commend her excellence as a homemaker; to admire her resolution and the care with which she surrounded those whom she loved. He never spoke of the tenderness which had been superseded by duty; the habit of loving which had lapsed as care had encroached upon their lives. If Lewis yearned for a small farm in the Wales of his childhood, where he and a young woman would bring up two children away from the memory of raised voices and the sound of blows thudding into unresisting flesh like objects dropped on sand, he never allowed his longing to overcome commonsense. The young woman on the farm was faceless; she had no name nor did he allow himself to place Anita Fielding explicitly in this middle-aged fantasy.

It was almost as if Dove had guessed the younger woman's thoughts and she slid the envelope towards Anita. 'We're having a small party at the weekend and I hoped you might be able to come. Quite informal, just to introduce my brother and his wife to our friends.'

'I . . . I'm not sure.' Anita stopped, trying desperately to find an excuse to avoid having to accept. 'What about the children? I don't like to leave them alone and . . .' her voice trailed into silence.

Dove turned and smiled at them. Freya was lining up her pens; darker to the left, lighter to the right, and, with equal concentration, Cody was picking his nose. 'Absolutely no problem, bring them along. If one of the girls can't keep an eye on them, I'm sure that Pender will.' Dove was determined there would be no escape and Anita felt dread settle on her, sightings of Maisie with her friends reminding her of school where she had been consigned to the remedial class and taught by a retired colonel to whom Enid Glazzard bore more than a passing resemblance.

'Thanks then, we'd love to come.' She made one last attempt, 'If Freya's asthma doesn't play up again.' A tiny, forlorn hope shamefully extinguished, that her child might be ill and they could all stay at home in the safety of the little flat with pizzas on their laps and Cilla Black on the television.

Dove stood up. 'Say goodbye to Mrs Courtney, you two.' Anita, anxious to be found not wanting, spoke more sharply than she intended and Dove murmuring not to bother them walked towards the outside staircase to add Twiglets, Iced Gems and 7-UP, to the shopping list she carried in her head.

Dove paused on the top step. '*Une pensée d'escalier*,' she said and watched with satisfaction the incomprehension on Anita's face. 'I nearly forgot – is there anything you want? Are you warm enough here? The curtains are rather thin and I expect I could find others that might do if you'd like them.'

Anita Fielding shook her head, blonde hair bouncing on her shoulders. Behind her Freya began to cough, a dry, brittle gasp preceding each painful expulsion of breath.

Anita turned around but Cody was already handing his sister her puffer and stood with his hand on her shoulder, the responsible expression of an adult on his face. Dove remembered Pender's words, *'he's a little cracker'*, and spoke more kindly to the woman watching her children as they stood together on the worn rug. 'I've a bigger carpet you can have as well: I'd forgotten that children like to play on the floor. We've only ever used these rooms for overnight guests, you see, or friends of the girls and it is a bit basic, I can see that.'

To Dove's confusion she saw tears shining in the younger woman's eyes. 'You're all so kind to us and you hardly know us really. If it hadn't been for Pender I don't know what would have happened when my husband left. He'd cleared out the bank account and taken the car and Pender was the only person I could think of who might help us.'

'Why ever should you have thought that?' Dove was still on the outside staircase and Anita pulled the door close so that the children couldn't hear her talking. It was cold, a wind full of rain rounding the corner and threatening the bushes as it passed. Dove knew it would seep into the room behind her through the inadequate curtains, and that draughts would infiltrate through the floorboards.

'Well,' Anita looked embarrassed. 'He'd flirted with me a bit. Oh, nothing heavy – a bit old-fashioned really, but I knew he liked me.' Anita's head nodded agreement with each word as if responding to some inner prompting. 'A lot of people, women mostly, are suspicious if you're blonde and, well, fairly attractive, and I couldn't think of anyone else to go to for help.' Her face looked pinched and Dove saw to her discomfiture that Anita Fielding was afraid. 'I was leaving Penalverne you see and if it'd just been me I'd have managed OK but it's different with children, isn't it? You can see what Freya's like and after all the upsets I'd have done anything to find somewhere we could stay for a bit and get ourselves sorted out again. Forget what it was like to be frightened all the time.'

'Frightened of what?' Dove hardly knew she had spoken.

'My husband. He was pretty nasty to all of us but Freya really seemed to annoy him when she started coughing and the more he shouted at her, the more she coughed. I was going to stay with my sister, although she hasn't really got any room for us, but I'm glad we're still in Penalverne because the children feel settled here and they like it by the sea.'

She stopped and Dove looked back through the crack in the door to where Cody and Freya were playing in the shabby, badly lit room behind her. She needed to know about Lewis; her husband who no longer seemed to be the acquiescent, approving consort who had surrendered to her stronger will almost by stealth until Dove hardly thought to consult him any longer. Rejerrah was her house, where she had reigned unchallenged until this commonplace little family had undermined everything she had fashioned in her own image, threatening to destroy what she had created over thirty years of what Dove had always believed to be a happy and successful marriage.

Dove looked at Anita's too-blue eyelids; at her hair which was too gold, too full of amateurish highlights; at the leggings and the sweatshirt with an exhortation on it, and said only, 'I'll send some things over, if that would suit you. I'll ask Jossy and Diana to help: no need to bother Pender or Lewis.' Dove turned and walked down the steps, now slippery with drizzle, and turned the corner towards the house before she allowed the angry, mortified tears to escape.

When Dove woke she felt no worse; not much better but less nauseous and her headache had diminished to a point where she could sit up and begin to think ahead. If she coughed or moved sharply a wave of queasiness swept over her so, very gingerly, she got out of bed and went to fetch a glass of water from the bathroom. Then she put two pillows upright against the bed head and leaned against them, eyes closed, until the room stopped moving.

Dove had been thankful that her migraines had lessened in number in middle age so the ferocity of this latest attack had taken her by surprise. It had followed a few days after her visit to Anita Fielding and preceded a few days of intensive preparation for the party. Dove, fretting at relinquishing control of her kitchen, had to ask Jossy and Loretta if they would take over the food. 'I've done the shopping – everything except the cream and extra milk, and that's got to be collected on Saturday morning – and lists of what to do, and when, are in my notebook.'

Almost at once Jossy had broken a cardinal rule and torn the pages covered in Dove's bold handwriting from their binding and stuck them with bits of ragged Sellotape to the doors of cupboards in the kitchen. When Dove discovered this desecration she had thrown the book into the back of a drawer and fetched another, still immaculate and undefiled, from the stock in her desk where they were concealed under a pile of re-useable envelopes, like an alcoholic's emergency supplies.

As a matter of principle over Luke's invitation, Diana had refused to help with any of the work, relenting only to make several puddings, the commission of which she had negotiated with Jossy for an evening to be spent baby-sitting. Diana intended to introduce Anita Fielding to several of her friends but allowed Dove no intimation at all as to her motives. Dove thought it to be a challenge to her authority but it was easier to acknowledge it publicly as altruism.

When Dove came downstairs on the evening of the

day before the party not only was everything ready – washed, counted, polished, stacked – but there was also the unmistakeable smell of pasties cooking for dinner.

'I made tiny pasties for tomorrow so I thought I might as well make bigger ones as well as they're Lawry's favourite. I hope you don't mind about me buying more meat.' Loretta looked at Dove and Dove saw that Loretta wouldn't mind at all whatever her objection might have been. She saw, too, that everything had been completed without her. Dove had heard laughter and music from time to time as the kitchen door was opened and had imagined – or perhaps she had dreamed it, she couldn't be sure – the sound of children's voices. Dove looked around the kitchen and forced herself to smile. 'What a good idea, although I'm not sure I can manage one yet. And thank you both, very much; it all looks absolutely super, I don't know what I'd have done without you.'

Sadly Dove Courtney pulled her lists from the cupboard doors, peeling off tenacious Sellotape and crumpling the paper, covered with obsolete instructions, in her suddenly shaky hands.

'Are you sure you feel up to going?' Enid was helping Girlie into a dress of dusky pink. She had chosen opal earrings and a large cabochon-shaped pendant of the same milky denseness shot with veins of scarlet fire and peacock trails. On her left hand was another opal, greener, and surrounded by diamonds, and on her right a moonstone.

'I want you to sell the opals, Enid. I've always been superstitious about them and I only wear them because Grenfell gave them to me and I shed all my tears for him long ago.' Enid knew Girlie was thinking of the reputation of opals for bringing tears with them; an irrationality persisting among the Cornish from the time when families were fractured by distance and necessity.

'If that's what you really want.' There was no more pretence between them, Girlie more frequently now instructing Enid in the disposition of her personal effects. 'Choose what you want for yourself and give the rest to Maisie's granddaughters. I thought Maisie, herself, would like this moonstone as it belonged to her mother.' Girlie spread out her hands; brown, speckled, and with newly varnished nails. She gave her small hiccupping laugh. 'An old woman's vanity, but I should hate to be seen unmanicured. As if it matters.'

'We all have our little conceits.' Enid looked up from

easing up the zip at the back of Girlie's dress. 'I've become very choosy about shoes since I realised that I had decent legs.' She smiled, 'All done. But you didn't answer my question – *do* you feel well enough to go?'

'Dear Enid, always so concerned for me. But don't worry I wouldn't miss this for the world. I was going to say, "if it's the last thing I do", but that seems like tempting fate.' Enid picked up a silver-spined comb from a set on the dressing table and began to arrange Girlie's hair. When she had finished to their mutual satisfaction, she put her hand on Girlie's shoulder, where Girlie covered it with her own good hand. The two friends looked at each other for a long time in the glass in front of them. It was silvery and foxed and they seemed like a photograph which has been left fading in the sun; faraway and diminishing into memory. At last Girlie said, 'You'd better go and get ready, Enid. Will you wear your burnt orange dress? It suits you so well.' As Enid turned towards the door Girlie spoke again. 'I'm ready you know, Enid. Quite ready.' Neither of them needed to pretend to misunderstand her words.

Girlie and Enid had been asked to arrive before the other guests and went straight to Maisie's front door. The lights were low and the familiar rooms smelled faintly of apples, as they always did. Pender opened the door to them: he was in his black and white trousers and a bow tie which, he felt, enhanced his resemblance to Maurice Chevalier. When he sat down two inches of cardinal red sock were apparent. He kissed the two women, managing to convey to Enid an enquiry about Girlie without speaking or breaking the flow of his good humoured chatter as he went with a sinking heart to pour their usual drinks.

Sandy sidled with embarrassment close to his former mistress, who stroked his head almost carelessly. Pender saw Enid looking at the dog. 'Been up and down more times than a tart's knickers.'

'What has?'

'Me and my foster-dog. To the vet. Arthritis.' Pender laughed and handed Enid a generous sherry. 'Both of us now, so that's all right. We can curtail our roaming to a sedate stroll and neither minds.'

'He loves it here with you: I could be jealous.'

Pender looked pleased. 'Glad to have him; bit of male company, you know. Dove hates him, of course, but Maisie and I have grown fond of the old rascal. We'd really like to adopt him officially wouldn't we, old thing?'

'Don't be ridiculous, Pen, Sandy's not a child. And talking of children,' Maisie turned to Girlie, 'Anita Fielding's bringing her children to the party. I can't imagine what Dove was thinking of asking her in the first place – and with her children as well.'

Enid glanced at Pender. He was admiring his magenta socks and wishing he had bought more of them while they had been reduced in the sale. He looked up, caught Enid's eye, but spoke directly to Maisie. 'Very canny of Dove, if you ask me. Told you she wouldn't give Lewis up without a struggle and by luring little Anita into the lion's den, children and all, she's been passing clever. After all, Dove's gambling for high stakes.'

No one spoke, Enid and Girlie assimilating Pender's words; sorting them into a relevance which gave meaning to their suspicions. At last Girlie said, 'We *did* wonder . . . we couldn't *quite* believe you were really interested in her, Pen: but *Lewis*!'

'Heard rumours, of course.' Enid sounded gruff with embarrassment. 'Didn't know what to believe, to tell the truth.'

Other cars were arriving, their headlights carving into the walls of the house; searchlights seeking truth in the corners of the quiet room, secrets betrayed. Maisie's voice sounded old and impeded by anxiety, forced out of her reluctantly. 'I can hardly believe it of Lewis – that he should hurt Dove so. She's been so good to all of us, absolutely selfless and now . . .' She stopped and Enid Glazzard, glancing at Pender, knew what would never be said.

'You think, do you Maisie, that Dove hopes that by seeing Lewis among his friends and family, it'll put this woman off?' Girlie was holding her drink, untouched, in her moonstoned hand and Enid was surprised that Girlie should have understood so clearly Dove's intention.

'To be fair,' Pender said, 'Anita never set her cap at Lewis. She'd had a rotten time with that husband of hers but even so, when she realised that Lewis was getting in deeper than he intended with her, she planned to leave Penalverne. Didn't want to be involved with a married man, you see. She is actually,' Pender said, 'a very moral woman.' He studied his glass and gave a short, unamused laugh. 'Because she stuck to her principles some of the men at the Yacht Club who'd tried it on with her and got nowhere started filthy rumours and it didn't take long for their poisonous wives to amuse themselves by spreading them further.'

'Eileen and Sybil.'

'Eileen and Sybil and that bloody Trundle woman.' Pender looked at Enid. 'I tried to help her, no strings attached . . .'

'. . . But being a silly old man,' Maisie interrupted and Pender looked at her before he spoke again.

'But, as my sister so rightly says, being a silly old man, I involved Lewis. Never thought for a moment, though, that it'd all get out of hand; that he'd fall for her and it'd lead to this trouble.'

'What trouble, Pender? We don't know what you're talking about.' Girlie was watching Pender for indications, learned over many years of friendship, that he wasn't telling the truth. She saw none.

'Well, don't want to say too much, but Dove's been very steely lately; bit unsympathetic all round.'

'You can hardly blame her.'

'Don't get me wrong, Enid, she's never wavered in her care of us but she's taken against Loretta in a big way and Lawry never could do anything right. Then, of course, Diana's home, *sans* husband, and Dove is absolutely not going to accept that.'

'Doesn't sound all that much different from usual – or shouldn't I say that?'

'One of the family now, Enid, say what you like.' Pender stood up. 'Refreshers all round, or shall we wait?' Enid handed him her glass and he went to refill it, noticing that Girlie had put her full glass on the table beside her. He glanced at Enid, who gave her head an almost imperceptible shake and Pender returned to his seat unaccountably apprehensive.

'I can't imagine Dove without Lewis.' Maisie's voice reached out to Girlie Eustace, seeking concurrence, needing confirmation. To her surprise Girlie gave her small, exhausted laugh.

'I can; oh, I can. Did I ever tell you,' Girlie said, 'what your mother told me long after Grenfell was dead, when everyone expected me to be casting about for a likely candidate as a husband?' Girlie looked at Maisie, her oldest friend, whose judgement she knew to be flawed but whose tolerance had always seemed to be constant.

Maisie shook her head and Girlie went on, 'She said to me, and I've never forgotten her exact words, "You know, my dear, some women who choose to live without a man are much happier that way – but that's a very well-kept secret."'

'And you think that Dove is a woman like that: like all of us, in fact?'

'I think she very well might be.'

*   *   *

Girlie Eustace entered Rejerrah on Grenfell Woodvine's arm. She wore a dress of blue silk, paler organza panels looped back to her waist revealing her narrow ankles and buckled satin shoes. On the hand which rested on Grenfell's arm was a moonstone ring which had belonged to Verena and which was now the symbol of Girlie's betrothal to Verena's elder son. Girlie Eustace was eighteen and dressed as a Dresden shepherdess at the party to celebrate her engagement.

Grenfell took her in his arms preparing to dance, when a tap on his shoulder made him turn. Pender, younger by six years and a toreador for the evening, stood there, covetous eyes on Girlie. 'My dance, brother: after all, you'll have her for the rest of your life.' And Girlie had floated away with Pender, hampered by the tightness of her skirt and her unwillingness to leave Grenfell's side. The music, she remembered, had been the 'Gold and Silver Waltz'.

It was the same toreador, older, less agile, who settled Girlie in a chair at Dove's party, away from the door but well-placed to be able to see all that was going on.

'I'll fetch you a coffee, shall I?'

'No, Pen, thank you, just a glass of water.'

'Fizzy or still?'

Girlie looked at him with amusement in her still merry blue eyes. 'Tap would do.'

When he brought it to her, Girlie delayed his departure with a hand on his. 'Do you remember the party we had to celebrate my engagement to Grenfell? You were Don José and I was a shepherdess and Grenfell wore his uniform. The last party . . .' She faltered and Pender patted her hand. 'I was remembering it all just now and it seemed so real that I could hardly believe it was over fifty years ago. I wonder sometimes if Grenfell would look like you now.'

'Not so much like Maurice Chevalier, I imagine: more James Stewart?'

Girlie laughed softly. 'You know, Pen, I've always thought that if we resembled anyone, you and I, it was Judy Garland and Mickey Rooney in those terrible old films: always so full of anticipation of good times and such hopeless enthusiasm.'

'"Let's stage the musical right here," you mean?'

'Something like that; gliding over the surface, always managing not quite to slip through the ice.'

The room was beginning to fill up, voices amplifying to the point where no single speaker could be identified, when the door opened again and Girlie saw Anita Fielding standing uncertainly with her two small children, half in and half out of the room.

Pender put his face close to Girlie's ear. 'Better go – might help to avoid a diplomatic incident.' Girlie smiled her understanding and Pender arrived beside the alien little trio at almost the same time as Dove.

Dove was welcoming, the gracious hostess drawing her unfamiliar new acquaintance into the Courtney circle. Anita looked around and saw faces which frightened her. They were confident and smooth, nourished by the best of everything from a cossetted childhood to a well-provided-for old age. Their clothes were the accepted uniform of good taste which only money could provide: voices burnished by indulgence, and the signs of age detained in a golden net of self-possession.

'*So* glad you could make it.' Dove grasped Anita's elbow, eyes flickering like a salamander's tongue as she took in the black dress with its badly machine-stitched hem, too short and just too tight so that it was beginning to wrinkle over the hips. 'Diana'll look after your little ones while I introduce you to people. Come along.'

Dove propelled Anita to the nearest group. 'Have you

met Anita Fielding? A friend of ours who's staying in the flat over the garage for a while.' Basil and Betty Sixsmith obligingly made room for Anita and Betty started on her well-practised social offensive. She was wearing a skirt of knife pleats in an expensive explosion of colour and on her silk blouse was pinned a brooch of such dazzling exuberance that Anita imagined it must be a fake.

'I can see that you're admiring my brooch.' Betty's apricot head swirled as her fingers twisted the jewel just enough for it to flash its message at Anita. 'Do you think that it's too much? I almost never wear it, of course, only on special occasions. But I said to Basil, "What occasion's more special than a party of Dove's," didn't I darling? And it was a good excuse to get it out of the bank. Anyway I'm comforted to see that you've chosen to sparkle as well.' Betty looked at the line of diamanté delineating Anita's neckline, caught Basil's eye and buried her face in her drink before turning the conversation to golf.

Pender had been sidetracked on his way to Anita's rescue but arrived in time to field Betty's next attempt at conversation. He greeted both women with every appearance of pleasure, sweeping Anita out of harm's way, whilst managing to convey amusement at something Basil had said.

'Come and meet someone much nicer,' he whispered and as Anita's head turned, looking for her children, 'they're in safe hands – my niece Diana's. She doesn't much like children so she's the best one to look after them.'

Anita looked unconvinced and Pender explained, 'Joke. Actually she's using them as a human shield to protect herself from her husband. She's just left him and thinks he's coming tonight, so she won't let the children out of her sight.'

'And is he coming?'

'Well now,' Pender was moving towards the corner where Girlie was sitting. 'As it happens, I was in Dove's kitchen and the only one available to answer when he telephoned his regret at having a previous engagement but, do you know, I believe I forgot to pass on the message.' He smiled his, almost, charming smile at her. 'Old age plays such tricks with the memory.'

Enid had moved a triangular shaped chair next to the armchair where Girlie sat upright, feet crossed at the ankles, her face slightly flushed, eyes curious. Enid stood up as Pender approached them and spoke kindly to Anita. Anita reminded Enid of a horse she had owned long ago; unprepossessing at first sight but which had turned into a reliable children's ride under her patient guidance.

'Sit here, my dear, and talk to Miss Eustace for a bit, she must be tired of me. You can tell her all about your children; we've heard such a lot about them from Pender.'

Anita sat down, grateful for the older woman's introduction. She always found it hard to initiate conversation but once primed had no difficulty in continuing to talk. Girlie had been watching Anita as she changed places with Enid and now smiled at the young woman. 'You're very pretty, Mrs Fielding, and we can do with a leavening of beauty, all of us wrinklies – I think that's the word you use nowadays? Tell me about Cody, won't you? He certainly seems to have endeared himself to Pender and I'd like to meet both your children. Perhaps you'll have a chance to introduce us later on.'

Girlie chattered on, sometimes fixing Anita Fielding with an ingenuous blue stare, sometimes watching her covertly with shrewd assessment. *Pretty, certainly. An air of vulnerability which might appeal to men, who would fail to recognise the tenacity concealed by the girlish manner. Rather prosaic conversation. Quite ordinary, really; someone of whom Lewis would tire quickly I'd have thought, and of whom Dove need have no lasting misgivings.* This was what Girlie Eustace told Maisie in the quietness of Maisie's apple-smelling house much later in the evening when the guests had gone home and they sat companionably together, dissecting the party over a nightcap.

Anita had been passed like a trophy amongst all the Courtneys' friends, as much an introduction to the family as was Loretta. Anita had never even begun to relax and would have left early, slipping thankfully back to the sanctuary of the tiny flat, except that each time she thought of leaving she failed to see Cody or Freya and to enquire as to their whereabouts seemed too daunting in the face of Dove's apparently confident assumption of Anita's own enjoyment.

The children had appeared briefly at supper time and Anita had watched, mortified and impotent, as they circled the table, filling their plates to overflowing.

'Good to see healthy appetites.' Maisie stood next to Anita now, restraining her by force of conversation from reaching her children. There was smothered laughter from some of Dove's friends but Diana, picking at crisps and celery sticks, encouraged the children to take French bread, joking with them as butter, softened in the heat of the room, dropped in greasy rivulets on to Dove's snowy white tablecloth. They scattered salad, fingered food which they didn't want and made disgusted faces at unrecognised titbits.

In one of those silences which falls on a crowd, when all conversation is suspended for a fraction of time and an angel passes by, Cody's thin, insistent voice sounded loudly in the stillness. 'This is *wicked*. Absolutely the dog's bollocks.'

The silence became more profound and Diana took Cody's plate, pushing him in front of her to the kitchen, hearing laughter close up the space behind them.

'*What* did you say? Wher*ever* did you hear that expression – as if I needed to ask.'

'Pender says it all the time.'

'Pender's a rude old man and it's not a nice thing for anyone to say, especially not a seven-year-old.'

'Do you want to know what else Pender says?'

'Not in the slightest, thank you.'

'Pender says,' Cody held a sausage roll above his head, whirring it around like an out of control 'plane. 'He says he's the light of my mother's life.' The sausage roll crash landed, pastry flying.

'Well, you horrible child, I'm afraid that your mother may shortly find herself scheduled for a power cut.'

'What d'you mean, Diana? Diana?' Cody put down a dripping vol-au-vent and looked at the girl in charge of him. 'I think Freya's going to be sick.'

Diana had forgotten the little girl in her necessarily concealed glee at the impact of Cody's words on the people gathered in the dining room. Now she looked around and saw Freya, pale and anxious, sitting at the kitchen table. She had cleared a little space for herself, pushing aside smeared glasses and unwashed plates to leave room for the arrangement of her food in a sensible order. When she had marshalled everything to her satisfaction, Freya realised that she wasn't hungry but, nevertheless, felt very unwell.

'It's prob'ly the cigarette smoke,' Cody said helpfully. 'It always makes her ill. She'll have asthma next I expect.' He bit into a meat patty and spat it out again immediately. 'Yuk, that's *disgusting*.'

'It's a pâté patty – too good for you. What should we do?'

'Get Mummy.'

'No,' Freya croaked. 'I'll be all right. I just didn't like it in there. It's too hot and smelly and everyone's shouting.'

'That's what happens at grown-up parties: they smoke, they drink and they shout.' Diana looked closely at Freya.

'Would you like a glass of milk and a biscuit?' The small, anxious face lightened and Freya nodded. Diana picked up the plate of party food and tipped everything into the bin kept for Dove's compost.

Lewis had not enjoyed the party either. He had realised too late that Dove was inviting people he hardly knew, whom she had met through her various charity activities.

'I thought this was supposed to be for family,' he had grumbled and remained unconvinced by Dove's explanation.

'As we won't be having a Christmas party this year I've had to invite everyone we owe hospitality to. Oh, and by the way Lewis, I've asked Mrs Fielding. She seems to figure so largely in our lives at the moment I felt I could hardly leave her out.'

'Dove!'

Dove looked at Lewis: beloved, beleaguered Lewis, and smiled to herself. She knew he would never leave her but a reminder of how much he owed her was necessary from time to time and she could see that he was disconcerted.

Lewis had watched Anita's propulsion through the massed ranks of Dove's acquaintances – and Dove had watched Lewis. Unheeded and unseen she had noted each change of emotion on his face: she had observed him greet Anita Fielding and noticed the way the children jumped and smiled around him, exposing the careful concealment of a formal handshake as duplicity.

It was the openness of the children which betrayed Lewis, and Dove wondered where he had learned such dissimulation, and how long ago. She had not thought him capable of the resolution necessary to conduct himself with the secrecy inescapable in the pursuit of an affair – Dove would never even give space in her mind to the word *relationship*. In fact, she had not thought of Lewis, deeply and wholeheartedly, for a long time and now she was afraid that it was too late.

When Freya had started to cough and scratch at her neck, Diana had gone to fetch Anita and had found her talking to Loretta. 'I'm afraid that Freya's starting an asthma attack. She's in the kitchen as I didn't want to bring her in here, it's too hot and smoky for her.'

Anita had stood up at once and hurried after Diana. 'I'll have to take her home. I'll just say goodbye to your mother and we'll go.'

'What about my father?'

Anita stood very still, watching Cody pile more food on to a plastic plate that Diana had found for him in one of the pantries. 'What about your father?' she said at last.

'Aren't you going to say goodbye to him as well?' Diana removed two half-eaten profiteroles from the top of Cody's booty and turned innocent eyes towards Anita. 'Or did you think I meant something quite different? No, don't bother to answer that: Bethan's right, I am a bitch and, in any case, I'm hardly the one to throw the first stone.' Diana helped Cody into his anorak, teasing him with the flapping sleeves and handing Freya's jacket to Anita. 'I'll come over for coffee tomorrow if that's OK – see how Freya is. If she's better perhaps we could go out somewhere for the day: lose them down a mine shaft or let Peg Leg Pascoe keel haul them before smuggling what's left of them off to Jamaicy.'

Cody shouted, 'Damn y'r eyes, yer landlubber,' and even Freya giggled.

'Pender again, I'm afraid,' Anita said and looked at Diana as she took the plate of carelessly stacked bits and pieces. 'Thanks, Di, you're so good with them. I don't understand . . . well, not my business is it?' She shepherded the children through the back door. The night air smelled sharp and cold and Freya began to cough again. 'See you tomorrow then, and thanks.'

When she had gone Diana sat down in the chair where Freya had been. It was still warm, as if the little, insubstantial girl had found something of herself to leave behind. Diana pulled a packet of cigarettes from her cardigan pocket; the torn, patched cardigan Dove wore for gardening and which Diana had put on over her one good dress, much to Dove's annoyance. Diana knew that she had a talent for children, that she would have made a good and a sensible mother, and now she allowed herself to think of Luke and how he longed for a family. She knew that she could never have told him the truth, that the abortion she had had at sixteen, long before she had met him and fallen in love, had been unexpectedly complicated and had lessened for ever the possibility of her being able to conceive.

A few days explained well enough as a shopping and theatre trip to Plymouth with Dove, and the little boy that Verena had so longed for was gone. Dove had been a reluctant and reticent accomplice in her daughter's decision and had buried under her usual diffusion of activity the remembrance of what Diana had done. Diana was not so easily deluded, growing remorse precluding her from ever being entirely whole again.

Much better, then, that Luke found someone else and blamed Diana only for her arbitrary desertion of him. Better still that she move away to where she could re-invent herself in the image that was emerging from the tumult in her mind. *Diana Southy, survivor of the latest conflict, brings you this report from the scene*, she thought and took a long, singeing drag of her cigarette, the smoke making her eyes smart and start to water. Or so she told Uncle Lawry when he wandered into the kitchen and sat down beside her.

'Had enough, sweetheart?' Diana nodded and dropped ash into the exact centre of a slice of cheesecake already becoming gummy and sour in the close air of the kitchen. 'You did a wonderful job; bit of a handful, were they?'

'No, not really: not until Freya started to wheeze, any-way. Have you heard her, Uncle Lawry? It's really awful, I'd be scared to death if I was Anita.' She indicated her cigarette with a smile. 'My first for absolutely *hours* as I couldn't smoke in front of them and I was gasping for one.' She inhaled and looked at her uncle again. 'Did it go well, d'you think, and did Loretta meet all the people she was supposed to? The food looked brilliant, thanks to her and Jossy – not that I saw much of anything, too busy stopping Cody from going completely overboard.' Diana smiled gleefully remembering Cody's enthusiasm in the dining room, but all she said was, 'I think he spends too much time with Uncle Pen, his language is terrible.'

'Nice little chap, though.'

'Nice little family.'

Lawry took her hand. 'It'll work out, sweetie. One of the few things I've learned in my passage through this vale of tears is to expect the worst, hope for the best and to be thankful if life dishes out something in between. Look at me; happier now than I've ever been, but it's been a bumpy old ride to get here.'

'Uncle Lawry, can I ask you something?'

'What, more words of wisdom? Not really my scene you know, leave that sort of thing to my betters.'

'Nothing like that.' Diana finished her cigarette and stubbed it out on the plate of cheesecake, a habit which infuriated Dove. 'Loretta's not too old to have children, is she?'

'No, got a few miles in her yet.'

'You make her sound like one of your old bangers.'

'Sorry, force of habit. Yes, Loretta could certainly have children. Why?'

'I wish you would have a boy and we could give Rejerrah to him. I think women have been in charge here long enough and I can't see the three of us ever agreeing to share it.'

'I'll tell Loretta what you say and we'll see if we can oblige.'

Dove heard laughter in the kitchen before she pushed open the door and saw her brother and her elder daughter scooping pâté out of a dish with their fingers, the air above Diana's head blue with curls of smoke which gave her silhouette on the wall a curious, Medusa-like hairstyle.

Lawry looked up. 'Everyone gone?'

'Maisie's taken her chums back for a nightcap, and that's just what I need – a nice cup of tea.'

Diana got up and plugged in the kettle, fetching mugs from the dresser. 'How many for?'

'All of us I expect – is that eight?'

'Bethan and Julius won't want PG Tips will they? They only drink some weedy brew of their own. Have you ever tried it? It tastes exactly like silage smells, goodness knows what it does to their innards.' Diana poured water into the big brown teapot and moved dishes and bowls from the table into the sink and on to the draining board. She fetched a bottle of milk and put it on the table. Loretta had just come into the kitchen and was hovering, her hand on the back of a chair and Diana said, 'Will you be mother, Loretta?' glancing with concealed collusion at Lawry.

Lewis followed Loretta, carrying a tray of empty bottles, which he would separate carefully according to their colour into cardboard boxes, ready to be taken to the recycling bins in the morning. 'Best party yet, cariad,' he said and Dove heard Richard Burton and knew it to be a lie.

The back door opened and coldness squeezed into the kitchen passage, gliding and seeping silently into the warmth, diluting the air like water. Jossy came in and the outside light snapped off behind her. She heard the voices in the kitchen, saw a rim of light around the door and decided that she would join the party post-mortem. Might as well tell them now, Jossy thought, and walked down towards her family.

'Hello, lovely girl.' Lewis was far from drunk but not yet absolutely sober. 'Saw your grandmother home, did you?'

'They're all having a cup of what Granny calls "Ovy", even Pender.' Jossy laughed. 'They look so sweet, like children being given a treat.'

'I thought Girlie looked absolutely terrible.' Loretta's observation was followed by a silence, which Loretta herself broke, softening the starkness of the words by adding, 'Not that I know what she's usually like, of course. It's just that I've seen that sort of parchment look too often not to know what it means. When I worked at Hawthorn Lodge,' she added.

'Well, that's telling it like it is,' Diana muttered but, after one look at Dove's face, no one else spoke.

Jossy glanced at her father before saying, 'Actually there's something I want to tell you all so I might as well do it now.' Dove, alerted, looked at her youngest daughter before turning to Lewis. He knows what it is, Dove thought, so why don't I? Why do I *never* know?

Jossy's hands were clamped tightly round her mug and from where she sat she could see both her parents. 'I've decided not to go to university after all. I'm sorry, Mum, but I'm really not bright enough and it's always been such a struggle to get the grades. I know you expected me to be clever like Di but I'm not and I never shall be.'

'What do you intend to do then, Jossy?' Dove's voice was surprisingly gentle. 'Do tell us.'

A flicker of a glance between the girl and her father. 'I'm going to stay with Bethan and Julius while I make up my mind, but I think I'd like to learn to be a decorator.'

'A decorator of *what*, for pity's sake?'

'People's houses. I don't mean an interior designer, that's not what I want – well, not unless people ask for ideas. No, what I want to do is painting and stripping and putting up wallpaper. I loved doing Granny's house and I'm good at it.'

'My house.' Dove's words were automatic but spoken so softly that only Lewis heard them, or thought that he did. More loudly Dove said, 'But why go to Bethan and Julius? You could work from here and I can't see you among that lot, Joss. Why not stay here where you can at least be comfortable? You'll soon get tired of their frightful food and never having enough hot water.'

'So that's what you really think of them is it? I've often wondered. But why stop there? Why not, *"All those welfare scroungers and their dirty children?"*'

'I've never said that: that's not fair, Lawry!'

'Well, whatever anyone says it won't change my mind. I'm leaving with them tomorrow.'

Lewis, watching his youngest, beloved daughter, willed her not to add, 'I'm sorry.'

Loretta put an arm around the girl. 'We'll come and see you lots and I think your uncle and I may be your very first customers. Shall we tell them, Lawry?'

'If you like. Go on then. Or shall I?' Lawry smiled at his wife and Dove followed his fond gaze with a feeling she didn't understand to be jealousy. Loretta's hair was still the colour that, were she a horse, would have been described as dun but she had swept it up into a rosette on top of her head and the shorter hairs escaping confinement, softened and made appealing the new style. Dove looked at Loretta more closely, recognising with an astonishment that caused her physical pain that Lawry's wife was wearing one of Verena's dresses that Dove had preserved after her grandmother's death. 'Your dress,' she said, 'Loretta, your dress.'

Loretta turned to Dove but before she could say anything, Diana spoke for her. 'Loretta didn't have anything suitable to wear tonight . . .'

'. . . Not much call for it at Hawthorn Lodge and the dress I bought for the holiday in France wouldn't have been nearly warm enough . . .'

'. . . And I remembered that you told me there were some old clothes of Great-Granny Verena's in the attic, and we found this. Doesn't Loretta look fabulous in it?'

Dove looked at the glowing chocolate-coloured velvet which enhanced Loretta's complexion, healthy and improved from hours spent walking in the open air with Lawry, and managed to say, 'It does suit you,' adding, with a tremendous effort of will, 'what were you going to tell us just now?'

Lawry leaned back in his chair. 'An evening for surprises, isn't it? Ours is – you tell them, sweetheart.'

'We're buying a house down near the promenade and we're going to look after a few old people there.' Loretta turned to Dove. 'You've been so good putting us up here, Dove, but we'll be out of your hair as soon as the sale goes through. We can live there while we do it up and then you can get back to normal.'

Dove Courtney wondered to herself: *what is normal? Is it normal to have a middle-aged husband infatuated, if not in love, with a young woman who can offer him, not a comfortable home and thirty years of devoted attention, but the discomfort and disadvantages of life with two young children, who aren't even his own? Is it normal, after years of unselfish concern to have your daughters act in such an underhand way that the whole pattern of their lives is changed and you know nothing of it? Is it normal,* Dove thought, *for your brother to marry a woman so unsuitable as to divide the family into those who approve of her and those who will never accept her?*

Dove turned to Lawry, ignoring Loretta completely. 'Not Bay View? Surely you're not buying Bay View?'

'That's it.'

'But it's in a terrible state: you'll need to spend thousands on it to make it habitable.'

'That's the only reason we can afford it and there are grants and we're prepared to put in lots of hard work ourselves.'

'But,' Dove looked directly at her brother. 'Where did you get the money to buy it? You said you were broke.'

'Dove, cariad, a man must have some secrets,' Lewis protested.

Dove ignored him. 'Well?'

It was Loretta, who never saw the need for dissimulation, who answered Dove. 'Pender lent us enough for the deposit and the rest's a bank loan.'

'But Pender hasn't any money either.'

Lawry gave a smile that was almost a laugh. 'But, Dove old dear, Pender has expectations, didn't you know? And, apart from that, the bank manager's a friend of his. It's good of you to worry about us, but we'll be all right.'

Diana lit another cigarette, blowing smoke upwards. 'Looks as if Rejerrah is going to be a bit empty then. Uncle Lawry and Loretta leaving; Jossy going to stay with Bethan, and me off to London.'

'You didn't tell us you were going to London.'

'Oh, didn't I? Must've forgotten.'

'But somebody's got to stay here so that I can go on holiday. It's all booked up and I can't cancel now. Who'll look after Maisie while I'm away? I was counting on you, Loretta, with a bit of help from Jossy. Lewis?' Dove turned towards him but Lewis was reading the label on a bottle of sherry and seemed totally absorbed.

The passing minutes seemed audible, only the clicking from the faulty clock on the cooker breaking the silence. Eventually Lewis put down the bottle. 'Looks as if you'll have to think of something else, cariad. I think what I should do – if you want my opinion that is – is to ask Loretta, very politely, if she would mind staying here to look after your mother while you're away. Maisie is, after all, and whether you like it or not, Loretta's mother-in-law.' Richard Burton was an almost physical presence in the kitchen.

Dove looked at Lewis as if she were seeing him for the first time in a long while. 'I think,' she said, 'that you have forfeited your right to organise my life.' There was a smothered laugh but Dove wasn't sure from whom, and she went on, 'In future I shall do as I like, spend what I want and go where I choose. I shall start by building a water garden and I shall start at once, so I suggest that you ask your,' Dove hesitated and then said, '*friend*, to move out. I shall expect her to be gone by the time I come back from my holiday.'

'What about your mother?' Lewis was unmoved.

'I'll arrange with an agency for someone to come in twice a day to see to her.'

'There's no need for that, Dove, I'll be happy to do it,' Loretta said quietly, 'I'm quite used to it, after all.'

'And I'll stay until you come back,' said Diana. 'Poor old Gran, we can't all just abandon her, can we?'

'Where are you going, Mummy?' Jossy asked. 'Italy again or on a tour like last time?'

'Actually,' Dove said, 'I'm going to New Zealand.'

'And where, if I may return the compliment, did *you* find the money for *that*?'

Dove smiled at last. 'I sold Verena's pearls. Enough for

the holiday and the water garden, since you ask.' She was back in charge and started to shuffle plates and mugs into a sort of order. Jossy stood up and went to one of the pantries for black bin liners in which to collect the debris of the evening.

12 ∫

Dove was on an aeroplane, her mind full of rain that bounced upwards in its undreamed of excess, and of glow-worms in the darkness of a cave; of arum lilies growing wild in fields of white angora goats; of ferns with ribs like thick, black water pipes; and of a room in a museum lined from floor to ceiling with photographs of dour, unyielding settlers from Scotland who had prospered in a land as far from their own as it was possible to find.

She knew from what had been left unsaid in her last telephone call home to make sure that Maisie was well and coping with Girlie Eustace's death, that Lewis had gone from Rejerrah; that he had severed the strands of thirty years and had left Penalverne with a woman who loved him as he was and to whom he would never have to feel inferior. Dove had gambled everything on the certainty of his affection and she had lost.

Now that Girlie has gone, Dove thought, looking out of the small window at clouds as thick and uniform as snow, *Maisie will need my attention more than ever so I'll suggest to her that next week perhaps she and Pender and Enid Glazzard would like to move their bridge afternoon to the main house. We'll have to change it from Thursday to Wednesday, of course, as I have my hospital committee on a Thursday afternoon, but I'm sure that they'll see the advantage of coming to me and they'll soon get used to it.*

As the aeroplane dipped and angled over hidden plains and forests and deep waters, Dove had a sudden memory of Matabele Jack. It was a long time since she had thought of her grandfather but now she heard his voice from long ago: *'If you ever meet a lion,'* he had said, *'what you have to do is stand your ground, look him straight in the eye and when he's near enough, quick as you like, reach into his mouth, catch hold of his tongue and go on pulling until he turns inside out. Never give you any more trouble after that.'*

Now Dove Courtney, a woman who had stood her ground to lions all her life and who, in time, would learn the well-kept secret, fumbled for the notebook and pen she kept to hand in the flight bag at her feet. She pulled down the table on the seat back in front of her and settled down, tentatively content, to make a list of everything that would need to be done when she got home.

* * *

SARAH HARRISON

THAT WAS THEN

Newly single, safe and sorted . . .

Eve's separation from Ian is amicable, her daughter Mel is a high-flier, and her son Ben, the apple of her eye, is the local charmer. She has a congenial job, good friends, and all the time in the world to improve her tennis. But passion is no respecter of plans, and Eve's chaste tranquillity, like Ben's boyhood teddy, is about to go out of the window with a vengeance. Because when sons grow up, mothers must too . . .

Praise for Sarah Harrison:

'believable and touching . . . Harrison's writing is lively, crisp [and] full of humour.' *The Times*

'moving and funny' *You magazine*

The author of twelve novels, Sarah Harrison has written several children's books, short stories, articles and scripts and is also a regular broadcaster on Radio 4. Her previous novels, LIFE AFTER LUNCH and FLOWERS WON'T FAX (Shortlisted for the 1997 RNA Award) are also available from Hodder & Stoughton.

HODDER AND STOUGHTON PAPERBACKS

A selection of bestsellers from Hodder and Stoughton

The Topiary Garden	Jill Roe	0 340 66070 8	£6.99	☐
That was Then	Sarah Harrison	0 340 70731 3	£6.99	☐
In the Heart of the Garden	Helene Wiggin	0 340 69571 4	£6.99	☐
The Trespassers	Pam Rhodes	0 340 71236 8	£5.99	☐
Kinvara	Christine Marion Fraser	0 340 70714 3	£5.99	☐
Defrosting Edmund	Nina Dufort	0 340 71682 7	£6.99	☐
The Bobbin Girls	Freda Lightfoot	0 340 67438 5	£5.99	☐
A Promise Given	Meg Hutchinson	0 340 69684 2	£5.99	☐

All Hodder & Stoughton books are available at your local bookshop or newsagent, or can be ordered direct from the publisher. Just tick the titles you want and fill in the form below. Prices and availability subject to change without notice.

Hodder & Stoughton Books, Cash Sales Department, Bookpoint, 39 Milton Park, Abingdon, OXON, OX14 4TD, UK. E-mail address: order@bookpoint.co.uk. If you have a credit card you may order by telephone – (01235) 400414.

Please enclose a cheque or postal order made payable to Bookpoint Ltd to the value of the cover price and allow the following for postage and packing:
UK & BFPO – £1.00 for the first book, 50p for the second book, and 30p for each additional book ordered up to a maximum charge of £3.00.
OVERSEAS & EIRE – £2.00 for the first book, £1.00 for the second book, and 50p for each additional book.

Name _____

Address _____

_____

_____

If you would prefer to pay by credit card, please complete:
Please debit my Visa/Access/Diner's Card/American Express (delete as applicable) card no:

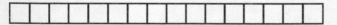

Signature _____

Expiry Date _____

If you would NOT like to receive further information on our products please tick the box. ☐